Synopsis

After Summer and her unborn Child survive the car accident Summer feels extremely blessed. Suddenly everything in her life feels great, that is until the shocking fact that Troy may be the father of Erica's baby comes to light. After everything they have been through Summer just doesn't know if her love for Troy outweighs her hate for Erica. Would it even be possible for Summer to be cordial to Erica, even for the sake of a baby or would it be problems on sight.

Shaq realized that chasing brighter pastures was hopeless without Summer in his life. Even with a whole family at home Summer still owned his heart and no one, not even Troy was changing that. Shaq is willing to risk it all to get Summer back even if it could cost him his life.

Troy is trying to leave the past in the past but when Shaq ignores his warnings he has a hard time. Dealing with the disrespect Shaq keeps throwing his way he has no choice but to go back to his old ways.

With all the drama Troy and Summer are trying to prepare for their babies' arrival while holding on to the little strength their relationship has left. Will Troy be able to get rid of Shaq once and for all and make Summer love him again? Will Erica's baby be Troy's and if it is can Summer and Erica get along for the children's sake? Find out when you read the second installment of Luvin' You is Wrong but it Feels so Right!

D0366012

Chapter 1

Shaq

When Erica told me she was indeed pregnant, and she didn't know if the baby was mine or Troy's, that shit fucked with a nigga. Here I was thinking I was going to get some pussy. If she weren't pregnant, I promised I would have jacked her little ass up. I knew her body was becoming thicker, but I didn't think shit about it. This hoe had played me in the worst way. I had to get the hell away from her ass. As I was driving back to the crib, I spotted Summer and her nigga. Now, I saw why Summer hadn't been answering her damn phone. She was trying to play wifey with a nigga who was playing her, too. The way they were laughing and enjoying each other pissed me off. They were going through a green light, so I pressed my foot on the gas, just enough to run into their asses. I knew what I was doing was wrong, but I didn't give a damn. She was supposed to be happy with me, not with his ass. When I bumped into them, I was able to get my car together and get ghost. I knew that once he found a nigga, he was going to kill my ass. That was when he found me.

Now that I had cooled down a little, I was heading back to Erica. We had to talk about this baby. She didn't lay down and have it on her own, so I knew there was a possibility it was mine. Calling Erica, I told her I would be back over in a minute. She sounded happy as hell. Making it over to her apartment, I stepped out of my ride. Looking both ways, I felt like someone was watching me. Making it to the door, I twisted the knob, and it was unlocked. When I made it inside, Erica was nowhere to be found. Damn, she just sat around with the door opened. She had to be crazy as hell. I made sure to lock the door before I headed over to her couch and sat down. I grabbed her remote and started flipping through the channels. It wasn't shit on, so I turned the TV off. A couple of minutes later, she walked out the room with a little-ass gown on; I could see all her curves.

"Damn, you just sit up in this bitch with the door unlocked. I could have been anybody walking up in this bitch." I frowned, and her ass laughed. I didn't see shit funny.

"Calm your ass down. When you called and told me you were on your way, I unlocked the door. I had to freshen up. I not too long ago woke up. What made you change your mind about coming back?" She was standing there, looking good as hell. I could have bent her ass over the chair, but I needed to explain myself. I was about to give her what she wanted to hear.

"I came back because I knew there was a possibility that this could be my child. It just fucked me up when you told me you didn't know if it was mine or his. Shit, you can't blame me for walking out."

"I know, and I am sorry. Like I told you, I feel like this child is yours. Troy and I weren't even fucking like that when I got pregnant, so that leaves you. I want us to be able to raise this child together, but I understand if you don't." She was still standing by the kitchen, talking to me. She looked scared. Getting up, I walked over to where she was standing.

"I'm sorry, baby. If this baby is mine, I will step up to the plate. Do you forgive me?" I whispered in her ear.

"Yeah, I forgive you. What in the hell happened to your face, though?" She touched my face, and I flinched, making a mental note to get checked out later. I didn't hit the steering wheel that hard, so I should be good.

"I'm good, you just worry about this dick. Come handle

this for me." I grabbed my dick.

Erica grabbed my hand and led me to her room. When we got in there, she pushed me on the bed and wasted no time swallowing my dick. My damn eyes rolled to the back of my head, and it took me no time to shoot my seeds down her throat. She swallowed and licked her lips. I was ready to get into her tight pussy.

While I was laying there, she tried to slide down on my dick, but I politely pushed her ass and retrieved a condom from my wallet. She looked at me like she was crazy, but I didn't give a damn. I wasn't even sure that this baby was mine yet, so what the fuck I look like fucking her raw? After I made sure the condom was on good, I pointed to my dick. Now she could bounce away.

"Girl, you better ride this dick. Don't act like you scared now." That little pep talk got her ass right, and she started popping that pussy on my dick. Her pussy was suffocating my dick, but I didn't mind, though. The way she was riding my shit, I thought I was about to bust.

"Damn, girl, slow your ass down. You better savor the moment. You know you won't be getting this dick like that no more." She slowed her ass up when I said that. It was the truth, though. If I couldn't get Summer back, I was just going to work on Monica and me.

"Oh my God, Shaq, this dick is so good, baby! Fuck, I'm about to cum all over this dick," she moaned, and that shit was sexy as fuck. While she was riding my dick, it was all hers. Once I left this bitch, it didn't belong to her anymore.

"Cum all over your dick then! Show the dick some love." Next thing I knew, she was wetting my dick. Damn, how I was going to miss this pussy. Tapping her on the ass, she climbed off my dick and arched her back just how I liked.

When I slid in, I bit my damn tongue. Erica's damn pussy was wetter than a motherfucker. While I was fucking her from the back, she threw her ass back. She was throwing it back, and I was matching it. I wasn't about to let her out fuck me. There was not a bitch bone in my body. A couple more deep strokes and I was filling the condom, but I wasn't done with that ass yet. I took off the old condom and placed another on my dick. Once I had it rolled down, I told her to lay on her back and let me show her a good time. She did as I said, and I was back inside her tunnel. I could fuck her all day, and the way her pussy was gushing, I knew she was enjoying it. Out of nowhere, she screamed and scared the shit out a nigga.

"Fuck, Daddy! I'm cumming!" she screamed. I was knocking all her walls down. After this, she wouldn't be able to walk right. I released and fell on the bed beside her.

All a nigga wanted to do was catch a quick nap, but I had other shit to do. Taking the condom off, I went to the bathroom and threw it into the toilet. When I walked back into the room, Erica was in bed, lightly snoring with her pillow between her legs. I had to laugh. I knew her shit was going to be sore for a while. Grabbing my pants, I put them on. Taking my phone out of my pocket, I saw that Monica had been calling me every five minutes. It was a little after one in the morning. Damn, a nigga was fucking up. I needed to get my shit together and be with only Monica. Hell, the way I went off on her, I doubt she wanted my ass like that anymore. Oh well, I still had Erica. Walking over to her, I kissed her on the forehead, and I was out the door.

When I made it out of Erica's apartment, Monica was calling again. I hoped that nothing was wrong with Ken. I started thinking the worst. Might as well go ahead and answer the phone.

"Yeah." I held my phone to my ear, trying to pull my pants up and get myself together.

"Shaq, where the hell are you? Ken and I have been worried sick about your ass!" she yelled into the phone. I thought it was kind of cute that she was worried about a nigga. She needed to turn that attitude all the way down, though. She knew I didn't play that shit. I didn't know why her ass was calling and flipping out on me anyway. She knew she didn't run shit around here.

"Man, I'm out. I'll be home in a little bit. I got some shit to handle, then I'll be on the way." I was tired of her ass questioning me. Why couldn't she just stay in her place? She stayed giving a nigga hell.

"Ummm, what the hell you gotta handle at one in the damn morning?" The shit reminded me of the time I started fucking with Erica and Summer called me. It was like Déjà vu, and I remembered that shit like it was yesterday.

"Man, gon' 'head on with that shit. I said I'll be home in a minute." She was pissing me the fuck off.

"Yeah, OK. Well, Ken and I are going to my mother's house so we might not be here when you get here. My mother wants Ken, and I want to spend some time with my mother." I took the phone from my ear and made sure I was talking to Monica. I didn't know who she thought she was fooling, but I knew better. She spent time with her mother every day, and we couldn't keep Ken from over her mama's house. Might as well say Ken had moved in with her. She had a room and everything.

"Be home when I get there, or that's your ass," I told her just before I hung up on her ass. She knew not to try me because she knew a nigga would spazz out on her ass. If she wasn't there when I got there, she was going to be sorry. I just hoped she didn't test my patience today. I was trying to be a better nigga for her.

Leaving out of Erica's apartment complex, I headed to the nearest gas station. Summer was heavy on a nigga's mind, and I had to make sure she was OK. I didn't give a fuck if her nigga died or not. When I made it to the convenient store, I located a spot to park. I had to get a blunt so I could get my mind right. Parking my car in the only available spot, I got out and made my way inside. Going to the register, I asked the clerk for a Swisher Sweets. Throwing a twenty on the counter, I told her to keep the change. I was now headed back out to my car until I heard someone talking about a wreck earlier. I stopped dead in my tracks and made my way back inside the store. Getting closer to the conversation, I stopped and acted like I was looking for something, knowing damn well I had everything I had come in here for, but I was a nosy nigga.

"Yeah, girl, they say the girl is in critical condition, and they say the baby didn't make it," one of the chicks said, popping her damn gum and patting her weave. Ghetto bitches were always gossiping. Bitches needed to learn how to keep their dick suckers closed.

I started feeling bad; I didn't mean for anything to happen to the baby. I was hoping that I could kill her nigga, and she would come running back into a nigga's arms.

"Damn, and I hope whoever hit them gets out of dodge because Troy is gonna kill whoever they are," the other chick said, looking just as ratchet as her friend. That was my cue to get my ass out of there.

Not wanting to hear any more of the conversation, I headed to my car. When I got in, I started breaking down the blunt. Pulling out the weed that I had stashed in my glove box, I dumped it in the empty blunt. Sealing the joint, I lit it up, letting the smoke hit my lungs. That shit was relaxing. I let my head fall back; this had been a hell of a day. Once I was good and high, I cranked up and proceeded to my next destination. I hoped like hell Monica didn't try a nigga tonight because the way I felt, I would snap her damn neck. I would take Ken and raise her on my own, and she wouldn't want for shit.

I tried my luck and headed over to the hospital. While driving there, I kept looking around. It felt like someone was watching me. I know by now, Troy had someone looking for me. Making it to the hospital, I saw him walking out of the hospital. I knew that I would get a chance to see her and make sure she was OK. Finding a parking spot, I parked and waited for him to leave. Once he was out of sight, I made my way inside. After I got the room number from the lady at the front, I proceeded to Summer's room. As soon as I made it to the door, I was about to walk in until I heard Carla's ass talking. I stood by the door and listened to their little conversation. I knew Carla didn't like me, but the feeling was mutual. Hearing enough, I left out the hospital. When I made it to my car, I peeled off. Now, I was going to take my ass home.

Chapter 2

Summer

I was confused as hell as I walked up to my mama and hugged her. I had missed her so much. Seeing her had me emotional. I had dreamed of seeing her, but I knew I wasn't dreaming. She was so pretty in her white dress, looking like an angel. I pinched myself, and that shit hurt like hell, so I knew I wasn't dreaming. Why was I here with her? Did I do something wrong?

"Hey, mama, I miss you so much." I kissed her on the cheek. She still looked just as pretty as I remembered. I felt the tears falling down my face, and she quickly wiped them away.

"Hey, baby, I missed you, too, but what are you doing here?" she asked, looking confused. I wondered the same thing. How did I end up here? I couldn't remember to save my life.

"I don't know, mama. I think it was just my time to come home." The reunion felt so right, and I didn't want it to end.

"No, baby, it's not your time to go yet. I need you to take care of my grandbabies. We have plenty of time to catch up later. I want you to enjoy your life, baby." She touched my belly. When she said grandbabies, I was confused as hell. Last I checked, there was only one baby, so I looked at her like she was crazy, but they always said a mother knew her child.

"OK, mama, I love you, and I'll see you later." I hugged her tight, and she hugged me tighter. I didn't want to let her go, but I knew she didn't want to see me like this. I saw it in her eyes that she was just as happy to see me.

"OK, baby, don't rush it!" she told me with tears in her eyes. She tried to hold them in, but she had failed miserably. Tears were running down her face, and I saw the sadness in her eyes. Walking over to her, I kissed her one last time.

I was awakened by the beeping of the machines that were hooked up to me. I started grabbing at the tubes because they were so uncomfortable in my throat. I didn't know what the hell was going on, but they needed to take these damn tubes out of my nose. They were burning the hell out of my nose. I was trying to snatch them out, but the more I snatched, the worse it burned.

"Oh my God, baby, are you OK?" Troy ran over to me and rubbed my forehead. "I'll get someone to take the tubes out. Hold on, baby." He ran out of the room to get help. It took him no time to come back with a doctor on his heels. He was becoming my rock. Troy had stepped up to the plate.

"Mrs. Jackson, my name is Dr. Wilson, and I have been caring for you while you were here. How are you feeling?" he asked as he took the tubes out my nose. I was better now that the tubes were out. I couldn't remember anything, and my damn head was throbbing. I needed answers.

My hands immediately went to my belly. I was in panic mode. They had me hooked up to a machine, and I heard multiple heartbeats. I looked around, confused. Why did I hear more than one heartbeat? I just sat there and waited for answers; this was too much for me. This was what my mama was talking about.

"Mrs. Jackson, I can assure you that your babies are good." When he said that, I looked at him like he was crazy. The last time I checked, we were only having one baby, but it was confirmed that I did hear a second heartbeat. I didn't know what was going on. Why didn't they catch it at my last appointment?

"Babies? The last time we checked, we were only having one. How many are we having?" I was firing off questions, and looking at Troy. He was standing out of the way with a smile on his face.

"Well, Miss Jackson, from the look of your chart, it looks like you guys are having twins." When he said that, it was like all the air was taken from me. I knew we would make great parents, but I was still scared. "Most likely, Baby B was hiding behind Baby A. If you all would like to know the sex of the babies, I can get a tech down here and check." I was so emotional at the moment, all I could do was cry. That was when Troy came over and held me tight. It had been confirmed that we had a set. Wow, this was amazing. Two lives were growing inside me.

Nodding my head, he paged an ultrasound tech to come to my room, and it took her no time to get there. It felt like she was waiting by the door. When she walked in, she introduced herself as Cary. She got to work, and when she was done, we found out that we were having a girl and a boy. Once Cary was done, she congratulated us, then she was out the door. The waterworks started again. I just wished my mother was here to see her grandbabies.

"Baby, it's gonna be all right. I know this is a lot on you right now, but I got you. No need to stress the babies out because I got y'all," Troy told me as he kissed my lips. Easy for him to say, I was the one carrying them. They weren't kicking him and carrying on, but I wouldn't change it for anything in the world. We had gotten into a heated kiss until the doctor butted in.

"Well, congratulations to you guys, and if you need

anything, feel free to call the nurses' station," he told us just as he walked out of the room.

"Wow, all of this is a shock to me. I can't believe we are about to be parents to two kids," I told Troy as I rubbed my stomach.

"I know, baby. I can't wait till they get here. We have our set, so if you wanna stop, it's up to you," Troy told me as he bent down to kiss my belly. This man was something else. I was glad that he had come into my life. He looked at me, and I knew he was about to start, so I mentally prepared myself. I already knew what was about to come out of his mouth before he said it.

"Baby, you know I gotta kill this motherfucker, right? He almost killed the kids and us. Once I find his ass, that's his ass." I saw the seriousness in Troy's eyes, so I knew for a fact that Shaq was good and dead. I was with it because if he let him stay alive, our lives would be miserable. I just didn't understand why he didn't want to see me happy.

"I know, baby. Do what you gotta do, but don't do anything stupid. The kids and I need you," I told him as I puckered my lips to get a kiss. That one kiss turned into a full-blown make-out session. We didn't come up for air until we heard someone clear their throat. Looking up, I saw it was Carla.

"Damn, y'all need to get a room," she laughed as she came over and hugged me.

"Bitch, this is our room, for now. Fuck you mean?" I gave her the side-eye.

"Well, OK, baby. I'm going out for a while to let you and Carla catch up. Do you need anything while I'm out?" he asked as he kissed me one last time.

"No, just hurry back to us. I miss you already." I blew him a kiss, and he left out the door.

"Y'all cute, I guess," Carla stated as she rolled her eyes. Her jealous ass. That wasn't a good look on her.

"Bitch, don't hate. You better get you a Troy," I laughed at her ass.

"Tell me what the fuck happened. Why is your ass in this bed? Is the baby OK?" She was cute firing off questions. You could tell she was pissed because her face was turning red.

"Yes, the babies are OK. Troy and I were on our way to view a house, and Shaq's dumb ass ran into us. He didn't even stop to see if I was OK. His ass just kept it pushing. He better hope Troy doesn't find his ass, though, because it's gonna be lights out for his ass," I told her in one breath.

"Damn, bitch, slow down. You said babies, and after that, everything was a blur. What do you mean, babies? I knew your ass was getting big as shit quick. What! Troy wasn't playing, was he!" she laughed.

She thought her ass was funny. "Yeah, they told us today that our daughter was hiding behind our son. I'm just as shocked as you are, so you can close your mouth," I told her, laughing.

"Damn, bitch, two kids at the same damn time. Y'all gonna have y'all hands full."

"I know, that's what I was telling Troy, and he told me that if I didn't want any more, we could stop. That's not the case, though, because I'll have all his babies," I told her honestly. I could see myself growing old with Troy, so none of the other stuff mattered to me. Shaq was dead to me, and once Troy found him, he was for sure taking his last breath.

"So, you're telling me that Shaq's dumb ass did this? He better hope Troy finds him before I do. I got a bullet with his name on it." Carla had a pissed off look on her face. Her face was turning all red and shit. I gotta love my sister, though.

It looked like something was bothering her, but I didn't want to bring it up. When she was ready, she would talk to me. Her eyes were sad, and I hoped like hell Sam hadn't done anything to my sister. If so, he would have to go through me. I would go to war over her red ass. I could promise him he didn't want these problems.

We talked for a little longer, and she told me she had to leave. I was OK with that because I was tired. These kids were draining me. She walked over to me and hugged me and promised she would call me later. As soon as she left, I drifted off to sleep. I didn't get much sleep with the nurses coming in and out my room. I couldn't wait until I was home in my own bed. This bed was so uncomfortable. I missed Troy like crazy, but I decided against calling him. I knew that any minute now, he would be walking back in.

Turning on the TV, I decided to check and see if anything was worth watching. While flipping through the channels, my babies started kicking up a storm. Placing my hand on my belly, I rubbed it a little bit. *Calm down, babies. Mama knows you guys are hungry.* I didn't want this nasty-ass hospital food, so I decided to call Troy and see if he would pick us something up on the way back.

"Hello. Everything all right, baby?" He answered on the first ring.

"Yes, baby, we're good, but we are kinda hungry, and I

don't want this hospital food." I poked my lips out like he could see me through the phone.

"Put your lips back in. What do you have a taste for? I can pick it up on the way back there." *How in the hell did he know I had my lips poked out?* Who was I kidding, Troy knew everything about me.

"I got a taste for chicken, greens, macaroni, yams, and I need a large tea, too," I told him, rubbing my belly. These kids had made me greedy as hell.

"Damn, baby, you gonna eat all that? My shorties 'bout to eat good," he laughed into the phone. He just didn't know I was about to give that food hell. I didn't even remember the last time I had eaten, so that was why they were kicking and causing a scene in there.

"Hurry up, baby, we are starving," I told him with a frown like he could see me.

"OK, baby, give me about forty-five minutes, and I'll be there. Stop all that pouting, with your spoiled ass."

"Whatever, I'll see you when you get here," I told him just before I hung up. I knew he was going to get in my ass when he got here. When we hung up with each other, we always said I love you, so me just hanging up wasn't a smart move. I knew he was pissed. Anyway, I was just going to enjoy the kids until Troy came back with our food. Rubbing my stomach, I let my head fall back on the pillow. I couldn't wait until these babies were out of me. I wasn't rushing it, but it was going to take time to get my body back to where it used to be. I was only six and a half months pregnant, so I still had a way to go. This was going to indeed be a long pregnancy.

Chapter 3

Troy

Heading out the hospital, I could have sworn I saw Shaq's bitch ass. Maybe my mind was playing tricks on my ass. His ass better stay in hiding. I decided to call Sam and see what he was up to. Pulling out my phone, I dialed him. Waiting for him to pick up, I headed to my car. I couldn't believe this nigga had the nerve to try and kill us. Shaq's bitch ass better look out because when I found him, I was putting a hot one in his head.

"What's good, my nigga?" Sam finally picked up.

"I can't call it, homie. Check this out, though. Where you at? We need to plan a murder." I was dead ass serious; this nigga was about to see me.

"You know I'm down for whatever. Pull up, I'm at the crib," Sam said just before he hung up. That was why I fucked with him, though; he was down for whatever. I didn't want to give him the details over the phone, but as soon as I got there, he was going to be all ears. Deciding to go since Carla was there with Summer was a good idea. I didn't want my baby there by herself since there was no telling where his ass was.

Pulling away from the hospital, I headed over to Sam's crib. He didn't stay far from the hospital. Pulling up to his crib, Sam was on the sidewalk, waiting. He didn't even give me time to stop before he hopped in the car. Pulling off, he started talking.

"What's good, nigga? Who we gotta murder? You know I'm 'bout that life." Sam stayed ready to murk a motherfucker. I had to laugh at his ass. He looked serious as fuck.

"Shit, I can't call it, man, but Summer's bitch-ass ex-boyfriend gotta go. So, we were riding over to the crib to look at it, and he hit us, and I thought Summer and the babies were gone. I came out with a couple of scrapes, but nothing major." I pointed to my head where I had the bruises. It wasn't shit to a G, I just had to make sure my babies were OK.

"Damn, nigga, run that back by me again. You said babies, as in more than one?" he laughed.

"Hell yeah, man. Summer and I 'bout to have two babies. The doctor said Baby B was hiding behind Baby A. That's right, her brother protecting her already. During the accident, I didn't think they were gonna make it. It was the scariest day of my life. When I find Shaq's ass, I'm telling you, I'm busting a cap in his ass," I told Sam, and he just shook his head.

"How do you know it was that nigga? It could have been someone else." I looked at his ass like he was crazy.

"Nigga, I'm telling you I know his car from anyone's car. Then the nigga got ghost. Pussy ass!" I was now hotter than a motherfucker. Just know his day was coming.

We rode around, looking for a bar. I needed a drink. One for finding out that I was about to be a daddy of twins, and I just really needed to calm my nerves. Pulling up to J and J Sports Bar, we got out and proceeded inside. There weren't many people in here because it was Wednesday. Sitting at the bar, I called the bartender over. She was a pretty chick, but right now, I had a wife and kids. When she made it over to me, I saw the lust in her eyes. What she had on was apparently too small, and her breasts were spilling out the top of the shirt. That shit looked ghetto as hell. I bet she thought she was the shit, too.

"Let me get a double shot of whiskey and whatever my bruh here wants," I told her, looking at her face. She wasn't a bad looking chick at all, but a little too light for my liking.

"What can I get for you, sexy?" she asked Sam, bending over the counter.

"First off, take your thirsty ass somewhere and brush your teeth. Breath smelling like ass and must. That shit is not cute, ma. Anyway, let me get a Bud Light." I was rolling at how Sam had gone off on the poor girl. I knew she was going to get it, though. I smelled her breath, and Sam was right. He could have come at her better than that, though.

"Damn, did you have to go in on her like that?" I asked, still laughing my ass off. Sam had no chill; whatever came to his head, he spoke it. That was my nigga, though, but I think his ass was dropped one too many times.

"You damn right. She came over here trying to be all cute and her breath smelling like that. You know how I roll, I don't sugarcoat shit. I bet she won't say shit else to us. Watch, she gonna come back, and her breath gonna smell like Winter fresh." He looked serious as shit.

"Nigga, you wild, but on a serious note, we need to get some niggas on the street to look for Shaq's ass. I don't want him dead right now, but I want him off the streets. He done fucked with the wrong nigga." Sam was sitting over there like he was thinking of a plan.

"No doubt. I will get some niggas on that. I wonder why he would do some shit like that. He must don't know our names speak volume in these streets." Hell, if he didn't know, he was about to find out sooner or later. Troy Davis or anyone close to him were not to be fucked with.

Ol' girl brought our drinks back and didn't say shit, but I didn't give a fuck. We sat there talking and plotting on how we were going to get this nigga. I knew that any minute now, Summer was going to call me. I was enjoying myself with Sam because I knew that once the babies got here, I wouldn't be able to go out like that. I was going to be on daddy duty. I didn't mind, though. I'd do anything for my family. I hadn't heard from Erica in a minute, so maybe she had found her real baby daddy because I knew she was fucking Shaq and me at the same time. I made a mental note to call and check on her tomorrow when I was with Summer. I didn't want to start any unnecessary problems. Speaking of my baby, she was calling me right now.

"Hey, baby, everything OK?" I asked her with concern in my voice.

"Yes, baby, everything is good, we are just a little hungry," she told me. I couldn't wait for my kids to get here. She knew I didn't mind getting them something to eat.

"OK, baby, what you wanna eat? I'll swing by on the way back."

"I got a taste for chicken, greens, macaroni, yams, and I need a large tea, too." My baby was greedy as hell, but I wouldn't dare tell her that. I knew the babies were making her eat more. I didn't care how big she got, as long as the kids were healthy. I was going to love her either way.

"Damn, baby, you gonna eat all that?" I asked her, laughing. My shorties were about to eat good.

"Hurry up, we're starving," she told me with a little too much attitude.

"OK, give me about forty-five minutes, and stop all that pouting shit, with ya spoiled ass."

"Whatever, I'll see you when you get here." She hung up in my face. Oh, I was about to get in her ass when I got there. She knew better than that. She knew I liked to hear I love you. She was spoiled like that because I spoiled her and let her get away with a lot of stuff.

"Sam, you 'bout ready to go? I gotta go feed my shorties." I looked over at Sam, and he looked pissy drunk.

"Yeah, I'm ready to go. I'm 'bout to go lay in some pussy," he told me, laughing. I was happy as hell he had found someone like Carla. She kept him sane and wasn't all about the money.

Getting up from the bar, we headed out to the car. Sam was drunk as hell. He was staggering all over the place, and I couldn't do anything but laugh. Once we got in the car, I headed to drop Sam off at the crib.

"Man, you OK over there? Laughing and shit to yourself." I couldn't do anything but laugh my-damn-self.

"Yeah, man, I'm straight. Ready to get home so I can get Carla to come over. This woman is it for me. Just thinking about her ass got my dick harder than a bitch." I shook my head at his ass; he had no damn chill. It was a quiet ride over to Sam's crib, and I guessed we were both caught up in our thoughts. Making it to his crib, we dapped each other and promised we would see each other later. After going to pick Summer up something to eat, I was now headed back to the hospital. Parking the car, I proceeded up to Summer's room.

When I made it to her room, she was knocked out. I wanted to wake her up, but I knew she was tired. Placing her plate down on the counter, I headed over and kissed her on her forehead. Bending down, I kissed her stomach two times; one for my son, and the other for my daughter. Summer stirred a little in her sleep, but she didn't wake up. Sitting there for another twenty minutes, she finally woke up.

"How long have you been here? Why didn't you wake me?" she started firing off questions. I knew she was mad, but I wanted her to get her rest.

"My bad, baby. I knew you were tired, so I decided to let you sleep." I walked over to her and placed a kiss on her lips.

"Thank you, baby, but I am hungry as hell; you should have woken me up." She stuck out her lip. I wasn't about to feed into that spoiled shit. I walked over to the counter and got the plate and placed it in the microwave. When the microwave beeped, I took it out and put it in front of Summer, and she wasted no time digging in.

"Damn, baby, slow down, that food ain't going nowhere," I told her, laughing at how she was inhaling her food.

"Shut up, we were hungry as hell, and you wanted to take all day to bring us something to eat," she fussed at me between bites. I was going to let her have that, though. I was just glad that everything had checked out good with them. She could fuss with me all she wanted to. Hanging out with Sam wasn't going to happen after the babies were born, so this time, I was enjoying every bit of it.

"I wanna know why you didn't tell me you loved me before you hung up earlier. You should know better by now. No matter how mad we are at each other, we still say it." I frowned at her ass. She knew I didn't play about that, but I knew she didn't mean it. Sitting there, I waited for her to finish eating.

"I'm sorry, baby, it's just that we were starving, and I wasn't thinking right," she told me just as she wiped her mouth. I guess she could get that.

"I'll let it slide this time, but don't let that happen again." I walked over to her and kissed her on the forehead. She nodded and got comfortable in the bed. I knew that once she got comfortable, she was going to be out.

"I love you, baby," she told me just before she closed her eyes.

"I love you more, baby. Check this out, though. I need to call and check on Erica. She might be carrying my child, too. I wanna get a DNA test before the child is born so I can know for sure," I told her honestly, and her eyes popped open. She looked like she was thoroughly rested when she sat up.

"That's fine with me. We can set up something with her. If the baby is yours, we need to file for custody. I think it will be better with us," Summer told me as she looked into my eyes. I knew she was mad because she said it with so much emphasis. I knew she was going to start some shit, but I didn't want to risk losing Summer again.

I didn't even bother telling Summer about the time she called me and told me that there was a possibility the child wasn't mine. Summer told me that her ass had called her and wanted to speak with me but she shut that shit down quick, telling her that she would relay the message. She didn't want that, so she called me. I was going to tell her, but we were in a good spot right now, and I didn't want to risk us falling out. She would probably understand, but the way her attitude was set up right now, she would snap on a nigga for breathing wrong, so I'd pass on that.

Chapter 4

Erica

When I woke up, Shaq was gone. Before he left, though, he had put a hurting on my kitty. I wanted us to be a family, but I knew better. The last I heard, he was running after the bitch Troy was with. I didn't know what was so special about her black ass. Who was I kidding, she was gorgeous. She had taken my man from me, so maybe I needed to take notes from her ass. Perhaps I could get and keep a man. Shaq seemed like he was going to step up and be a man if this was his child but only time would tell.

Looking over at the clock, it was a little after ten, and I didn't have anything to do until 2:15. Deciding to lay back down, I didn't wake back up until a little after one. I swear my body was so damn tired. If this was what it felt like, I wasn't getting pregnant again. I didn't like that I was doing this alone. Rolling out of bed, I made my way inside the bathroom. Rubbing my belly, I looked in the mirror, and I didn't like the person I saw. I was now almost six months pregnant and felt like a whale. I was always emotional, crying about any and everything. I broke a nail, and I started crying. This little girl was getting the best of me. Feeling her kick me, I knew she was ready to eat. Hell, I didn't remember eating yesterday.

"OK, mama's baby, I'm about to get myself together and get you something to eat." I rubbed and talked to my belly. This little girl was the only person who kept me sane. Everyone else could kiss my ass. As long as I had her, that was all I needed. I didn't need a man to keep me happy. As long as I could get some good dick from somewhere, I was good.

While I was in the bathroom, I turned the shower on. While the water was getting to the proper temperature, I washed my face and brushed my teeth. Once the water was hot enough, I stepped in and let the water run down my body; it relaxed me. Slipping my hands in front of me, I massaged my pearl. Sticking two fingers in and out of me, I let out a moan. Rubbing faster, I felt my orgasm rise. Next thing I knew, I was cumming all over my fingers. Leaning against the wall, I just stood there, trying to catch my breath. All I wanted to do now was sleep. Washing and rinsing my body a couple of times, I finally got out. Wrapping the towel around my body, I headed back to the room to find something to wear today. I had a doctor's appointment at 2:15, and after that, I was going to take a much-needed nap. I needed a massage, so maybe I would get one after I left the doctor's office. That sounded like a plan.

Grabbing the lotion off the counter, I started lotioning my body. Deciding to put on my white sundress, I slipped my feet into a pair of gold thong sandals. Spraying pure seduction body spray on, I peeked in the mirror. I must say, I was fine as hell. Grabbing my purse, I left out of my room. Heading to the elevator, I stepped in. When I got on, there was a fine brother on there. Hitting one, I waited for it to get to my floor.

"Hey, pretty lady, what's your name?"

"Erica, what about yourself?" He was a cutie. He was light skinned, tall, with a low haircut, and a full beard. All kinds of thoughts went through my head about his beard. I had to clench my legs.

"Matthew, but everyone calls me Matt. How 'bout I take you out to dinner? I know you can eat," he told me, looking down at my belly. Niggas were so rude these days. I knew I looked like I was about to pop, but damn, he didn't have to remind me.

Laughing, I told him I would pass. As soon as the elevator beeped, I hurried and got off. The nerve of this nigga. Making my way to my car, I felt my cell phone vibrate in my purse. Digging through my bag, I located it and answered.

"Hello?" I said it kind of rude, but I didn't mean anything by it.

"Damn, who pissed in your cereal this morning? I was calling to check on you and the baby." It was kind of cute, but he had made it known that he didn't want to be with the baby and me.

"We're good, but didn't you make it clear that you didn't wanna be with the baby or me? Go ahead and go be with your other baby mom." I was angry with him because he had thrown away five years for some bitch he had just met.

"There's no doubt about whether I'm gonna be with Summer, but I was wondering if we could set a date and time so I could get a DNA test done." The nerve of this man. I didn't need him to be in my daughter's life. I could take care of her on my own.

"Yeah, I can do that. Meet me at the doctor's office at 2:15 so we can get this over with." I was tired of dealing with his ass; he was either going to be in her life or not. I knew this child wasn't his, but he didn't need to know that.

"I can't come today because Summer is in the hospital, but we can plan something for a later date." This man had me so fucked up, it didn't make any sense.

"You know what, Troy? You and Summer have a good life. This baby and I can do without you," I told him, hanging up the phone.

Making my way to the car, I dialed Shaq. I knew his ass was going to give me hell, but I decided to try my luck.

"Yeah," he answered. This man was so damn rude.

"Is that the way you answer for the mother of your child?" I asked, and he laughed.

"You listen here, you little bitch. Until I get a DNA test, that damn baby is not mine. Is that clear?" I was hurt, and I couldn't fight the tears that fell from my eyes.

"Crystal clear," I told him as I hung up. Deadbeat piece of shit.

Hitting my hands on the steering wheel, I saw red. I wanted to kill Troy and Shaq. They didn't deserve to stay on this earth any longer. I was about to plan ways to kill their asses. "Sorry son of a bitch!" I screamed as the tears kept falling. I thought we were good, but apparently, I was just a fuck.

Girl, you knew this was gonna happen when you were sleeping with both of those men, so I don't understand why you're mad, the voices in my head told me.

AH! Leave me the hell alone. Stop talking to me! I pulled my hair and screamed. The voices in my head were getting worse. I had been diagnosed with dissociative identity disorder when I was fifteen years old. When I turned twenty-two, it got worse, and the doctors put me on medication, but I refused to take it. When I took it, it made me crazy. No one but my parents knew I had this disorder, and I knew if my sister found out, she would call me crazy for sure.

Man up and do what the hell you gotta do. They don't love

you, and no man will ever love you. You are a weak person, and you won't be capable of taking care of that child, the voices in my head told me. That made me mad, and I started hitting myself in the head.

Shut the hell up and leave me the hell alone. You don't know what you are talking about. I was having a conversation with myself. People were walking by my car, staring, but I didn't care, though. There was a knock at my window, and looking at the window, it was the staff from the hotel.

"Is everything OK, ma'am? Do you need me to call someone for you?" she asked, looking concerned.

"No, I'm fine. I'm on the way to the doctor's office. I should be back a little later." I rolled my window up and started my car. Heading to the doctor, I decided to listen to the radio to get my mind off things. Turning on the radio, K Michelle's song "Cry" came on. I decided to sing along with her.

I've learned from the best, I've learned from you
It's easy to do the shit that you do
I could just switch it up on ya
Used to be me, that was out here stressing
So give what came and cares
Now you missed your blessings
You gone suffer, you gone suffer
For everything you did
I'm not bitter, stay with her
Maybe she can take your shit

Once the song ended, my face was full of tears. I was hurt, and I had brought it on myself. Pulling up in the parking lot, I opened the mirror to look at my face, and it was puffy. Pulling out my makeup, I applied a little to hide the bags under my eyes. Feeling satisfied, I got out the car and headed to the office. When I got in there, I signed in and took a seat until my name was called. It wasn't a long wait at all, so I was called back in ten minutes.

"Good afternoon, Erica, my name is Dr. Swan, and I will be caring for you today. Are you having any problems?" she asked.

"No, I'm well. How is my baby doing, though?" I asked. I wasn't worried about myself, I was worried about my baby. "You have an ultrasound today, and as soon as that is done, I will come back in and talk to you. Sit tight, and the tech will be in shortly to take you back."

"Thank you, ma'am!" I told her as she walked out of the room.

I got the results of my baby's Down Syndrome test, and it looked like I would have a child with an illness. It didn't matter though because I would love her either way. I knew it was going to take a little more to care for her, but I was down for the ride. I didn't need a man to help take care of my child. As long as she had me, that was all she needed. When she grew up and asked about her father, then I would tell her the truth, but for right now, it was going to be just us.

Sitting in the room for about thirty minutes, Shelly, the ultrasound tech, came in and took me back. Making it to the room, the tech asked me to lay on the table. Laying back on the table, Shelly put the gel on my stomach. Moving the probe all around my stomach, she finally found my daughter. She was in a ball in my stomach, and her face looked a little weird.

"Shelly, is her face supposed to look like that?" I asked curiously.

"Erica, babies with Down Syndrome look like that. She looks like she is going to be beautiful, though," she told me. I felt a lone tear fall, but I quickly wiped it away. I didn't care, I was still going to love my baby.

"OK, we are all done here. I will take you back to your room, and the doctor will come in and talk to you," Shelly told me as she cleaned the gel off my belly. Getting off the table, I headed back to the room that I was initially in. Sitting there for a little while, Dr. Swan came back in the room.

"So, looking over your test results, it looks as if your baby has Down Syndrome, and we have options if you don't want her." The nerve of this bitch.

"So, you telling me that I could terminate my child because she has an illness? You know what, you can go to hell. I won't be terminating my child. I'm gonna love my child no matter what."

"I wasn't saying that. Plenty of adults out there can care for a child like yours. I would never tell you to abort your child, I was just giving you an option. I'm sorry if you took it the wrong way. It's a little too late for you to have an abortion anyway."

What she said made sense, but I wasn't giving my child up. I got up and stormed out the room. I didn't even schedule my next appointment. All I wanted to do was get something to eat and go to sleep. Today had drained me.

Chapter 5

Shaq

After leaving the hospital, I decided to go home. I wasn't really in the mood for Monica's bitching, but I might as well get it over with. Getting in my car, I started it up. While headed to the house, I decided to call Monica and see if she needed anything. I was trying to get back on her good side. I knew I might not be the best nigga for her, but I needed her. If I couldn't have Summer, I indeed wanted her. She and Ken were the best thing that had happened to me. Dialing her number, I waited for her to pick up.

"Yes, Shaq, what do you want? This is not where you wanna be. You told me you were coming home an hour ago," she told me with a little too much attitude. She had better calm all that down before I snapped on her ass.

"First off, calm all that shit down and take the attitude out your voice. I was calling to see if your ass needed anything while I was out. It seems like all you wanna do now is argue. Fuck is wrong with you?" I said in one breath. She was pissing me off, she just didn't know it.

"Ken needs some more pull-ups, and we are out of milk and bread. Do you mind picking that up?" I had to take the phone away from my ear and look and see who the hell I had called.

"Monica, cut all that shit out. I called your ass to see if you needed anything, so why the fuck would I mind getting it? I'm not about to sit here and argue with you. Have that pussy ready for me when I get there," I told her before I hung up.

Heading over to Walmart to get the stuff she needed, I

didn't know if I was being paranoid, but I felt someone following me. Every time I turned, they turned. I knew Troy would be looking for me, but not this damn soon. I made a quick left, and they kept straight. I needed to get to Walmart and get this shit so I could go to my mama's house and hideout. I wasn't ready to die yet; I had Ken and possibly another baby on the way. I knew deep down that Erica's baby was mine, but I wanted to be for sure.

Finally making it to Walmart, I hurried inside to get what I needed. Picking up everything I needed, I headed to the checkout. It took me ten minutes tops to get in and out. Making my way to the house, I had to mentally prepare myself. Counting to ten in my head, I pulled into the driveway.

Pulling myself out the car, I grabbed the bags and headed to the door. Putting my key in the hole, I twisted it and let myself in. It was quiet as shit. I knew Ken was taking a nap, but where the hell was her mother? Dropping the bags off in the kitchen, I headed upstairs. Entering my daughter's room, she was in her bed, sleeping so peacefully. I walked over to her bed and kissed her on the cheek. I wanted to wake her up, but I decided against it. We would play when she got up. Leaving out her room, I made sure I left the door cracked. Making my way to my room, I twisted the knob, ready to enter, but I decided against it. Monica was on the phone, and it was on speaker phone.

"Monica, I don't know why you put up with Shaq's ass. You know you can do so much better. Don't even start that shit 'bout he's Ken's daddy. Hell, y'all can co-parent." Her ratchet-ass friend Veronica was fussing. I didn't know why they were still friends when I had told her that she had tried to give me the pussy, but women were different than men.

"I know, girl. I'm gonna give us one more try, and after

that, I'm gone." I started to burst into the room, but Veronica started again.

"Girl, how many times you done said one more try, and that's it? That's on you, but when he breaks your damn heart, don't come crying to me. Once a dog, always a dog. You know I love you, but that's on you," she told her and hung up.

Entering the room, Monica was laying on her stomach. The sight in front of me was pretty as shit. She had on boy shorts and a tank top and her ass was eating those shorts. Walking over to her, I slapped her on the ass. The way her ass jiggled had my dick rock hard.

"Damn, nigga, why you slapped me on my ass like that? Shit hurt like hell with yo' heavy-handed ass," she fussed.

"My bad, baby. Let me kiss it and make it feel better." I was dead ass serious.

"Naw, I'll pass on that. What the hell took you so long?" Here we go with this shit.

"The store was busy, that's what took me so damn long. What I tell you about questioning me? And why aren't you naked? I told you to have that pussy waiting for me." I grabbed a handful of her pussy.

"Naw, Shaq, you won't be getting any more of this good until you get your shit together." She slapped my hand away. She had me fucked up, though. I was getting it voluntary or involuntary. She had a choice.

"Now you know I got that little pussy on lock. Ain't no way you're gonna keep it from me. I bet you wetter than a motherfucker." I cracked up laughing. It was the truth, though. She couldn't keep that pussy away from me. I didn't even know why she was fronting like she could go without.

I was going to let her have that, though. I made my way to the bathroom and turned on the shower. Allowing it to get to the right temperature, I took a piss. Once I was done, I stripped out of my clothes and entered the shower. Not even five minutes into my shower, I heard the bathroom door open. Peeping through the curtain, I saw Monica standing there buck booty naked. My dick was already hard, but she had made it harder. She walked over to the tub and got in. I didn't even give her a chance to get all the way in before I pushed her up against the wall. While she was pinned against the wall, I could hear that her breathing was shallow. Just as I expected, when I rubbed between her legs, she was wet as shit. Continuing to rub between her legs, she started moaning softly. She had her eyes closed, and she knew I didn't like that shit.

"Open up your eyes, baby," I whispered in her ear, and her eyes popped open.

"Oh my God, baby, I'm about to cum." Her body started jerking.

"That's right, let that shit go, baby!" I coached her.

Sex with Monica was never boring. She liked to try different stuff, and not only in the bedroom. I could get it wherever, whenever; it didn't matter the place. Hell, if we were at the grocery store and my dick got hard, you better believe we were going to the bathroom to handle it. She never denied me sex. If it was late and I was in need, she rolled over just to satisfy me. I loved that about her. Summer didn't hold a candle to Monica. Monica was stealing my heart more and more as the days went by.

Getting ourselves together, I went to Ken's room to check on her. She was still knocked out. I had to check for a pulse to make sure she was still breathing. She never really slept this long. Usually, she was up and playing. I was going to wake her, but I decided against it. I knew within a matter of minutes, she would be up, so I was going to spend some time with her mama. Kissing her on the cheek, I walked out of her room and shut the door. Making my way back inside my room, Monica was lying in the middle of the bed, naked. I swear that ass was sitting up. Moving close to her, I climbed into the bed on top of her.

"No, Shaq, get off me. I'm tired. I just need a nap before Ken wakes up," she told me in a sleepy voice.

"OK, cool. I'll let you have that, but tonight, I want you to suck the skin off this dick," I told her, climbing off the bed.

"You know I got you, daddy," she said as I walked out the room.

Going to the kitchen, I opened the refrigerator and got a beer. I popped the top on it and turned it up. Making my way to the living room, I grabbed the remote and started scrolling through the channels. Nowadays, there wasn't anything on TV. I decided to watch *Madea's Big Happy Family* since I hadn't seen it in a long time. I swear every time I watched it, I laughed more. Not even thirty minutes into the movie, I heard little footsteps coming downstairs.

"Daddy!" My princess came over and jumped into my lap. I swear I would kill for this little girl.

"Hey, daddy's baby. Did you sleep good?" I asked, wiping the slobber from the corner of her mouth. This little girl was just like her mother.

"Yes, daddy, I slept for a long time. I guess I was tired from playing at Grandma's house," she told me, stretching.

"Ken, are you hungry?" I asked, picking her up, heading to the kitchen.

"Yes, sir, can I have some cereal?" she asked with sad, puppy dog eyes. She knew we didn't give her cereal in the middle of the day, but because she was so cute, I decided to give in.

"Yeah, but don't tell your mom or we will both be in trouble," I told her, putting her down to get the cereal out the cabinet. Grabbing a bowl out the cabinet as well, I made Ken a bowl of Lucky Charms. Getting the milk from the fridge, I poured just a little into her bowl. She wasn't much of a milk drinker. I placed her at the table in her booster chair and put her cereal in front of her.

"Shaq, what I tell you about feeding her cereal in the middle of the day? That's why she's always hungry." Monica came in the kitchen, fussing. Monica looked good as hell with her nightgown on, and I knew she didn't have anything on under it.

"Calm down, baby, she was hungry, and cereal was quick. I'll make sure she eats later on," I told her, walking up to her and kissing her on the lips.

Walking over to the fridge, Monica took out the hamburger meat. She walked up to the sink and washed her hands. Grabbing a skillet from the dishwasher, she started cooking the ground beef.

"Baby, what are you cooking for dinner tonight?" I asked, walking up behind her.

"Shaq, get your nasty ass off me. I know you see Ken over there. I'm cooking nachos for dinner, though."

"Cool, that's what's up. Do your thing, baby. Ken and I

will be in the living room, watching TV. You ready, princess?" I grabbed her bowl and placed it in the sink.

"Yes, sir. Can we watch cartoons, please?" she asked with her lips poked out. She knew I was a sucker for her sad faces.

"We can watch whatever you want, princess," I told her, picking her up from her chair.

"Yayyyyy, cartoons!" She was too hype.

Making our way into the living room, the doorbell rang. I was paranoid than a motherfucker. Going over to the door, I peeked out the peephole, feeling relieved. It was only Ms. Sonja, Monica's mom. Opening the door, Ken almost jumped out of my arms.

"Grandma!" she screamed like she hadn't seen her in years.

"Hey, grandma's baby. What y'all in here cooking? It smells good as hell in here," she said to no one in particular.

"Hey, Ms. Sonja. How have you been? You know yo' daughter is in there, throwing down." I walked over to her and hugged her.

"I been all right. I was missing my grandbaby, so I decided to come over and see her," she told me, walking into the kitchen.

"Ms. Sonja, you just saw her a little while ago," I laughed as I closed the door. While I was closing it, I saw a car across the street that wasn't usually there. Maybe someone was watching me. I didn't know, but whoever it was, they had better come correct. Locking the door, I headed to the kitchen. When I made it in there, Monica was done cooking and fixing my plate. I was hungry than a motherfucker.

Walking over to Monica, she handed me my plate.

"Thank you, baby!" I kissed her lips. Sitting at the table, I said my grace and dug in. These nachos were the bomb. Once everyone got what they wanted, I was going to finish it off.

"You're welcome, baby. Me and Ken about to head to Mama's house for a while. We shouldn't be long. I'll call you on the way back." She kissed my lips.

"OK, hurry back!" I slapped her on the ass.

"Stop being nasty. Come on, Ken, and tell your daddy bye."

Ken came running into the kitchen and reached up for me. I picked her up and kissed her on the cheek. "Take care of Mama for me, OK?"

"Yes, sir. I'll see you when we get back." She put her little hands on my face and gave me a wet kiss on my cheek. "OK, y'all have fun. Daddy 'bout to take a nap."

Once they headed out the door, the car that I had seen earlier was still parked in the same spot. When I made sure they were in the car, I jogged back to the house. Once inside, I made sure to lock up and peeped out the window. It was like the person was looking at my place. I didn't know what the hell was going on, but I would figure something out when I woke up from my nap. A nigga was tired. As soon as I got comfortable on the couch, it took me no time to drift off to sleep.

Chapter 6

Monica

One thing I know, Mama didn't raise a fool. All the money Shaq gave me to go shopping, I put it in my account for rainy days. We had an account together, but I thought it was a good idea for me to have my own account. A lot of y'all don't know me, but my name is Monica Freeman, born and raised in Atlanta, GA. I'm about 5'8, caramel Barbie, slim waist, B-cup breasts and a ghetto booty. I wear long weaves but don't get it twisted, I'm not baldheaded by a long shot, I just love weave. Hell, my hair is just as long as my weave, I just hate to do it. I'm thirty years old, and I moved to Detroit because I had gotten in trouble in Atlanta. I'd had a wild life. My old boyfriend Fred and I got caught up with check fraud. We were addicted to the fast money, and fast money landed me in jail for a year. That was the most miserable year of my life. My family didn't mess with me, so I didn't have anyone. When I got out, I felt like I needed to change my life.

I had everything a girl could ask for. When I moved to Detroit, I met Shaq, and he changed my life. Even though he was only selling nickel and dime bags of weed, he made sure I had everything I needed. The craziest thing about it, he didn't even know me and moved me in his house. One thing led to another, and I got pregnant with Kennedy. Of course, when I told him, he wasn't pleased about it, but he took full responsibility for raising our daughter. We weren't struggling, but I felt like I needed my own money. When I told him I wanted to work, he flipped out on me, telling me no woman of his was going to be working. That was OK with me, so I sat my fine ass at home and made sure Ken was good. I knew Shaq was still trying to get back with his ex, but I didn't give a damn. He was doing him, and I was doing me.

Recently, I had met this fine-ass nigga named Craig, and we had been kicking it heavily. He was everything I wanted in a man. Craig is a 6'3, two-hundred-and-thirty-pound chocolate god. He looked like he was in the gym morning, noon and night. I didn't know what the dick was like yet, but he walked like he was working with a monster.

Craig had let me know that he was in the game, and I immediately thought about Shaq. He was bigger than Shaq, though. He didn't work on the corners or anything, but baby was bringing in the cake. When we started talking, I did let him know I was involved with someone, but he told me we were chilling right now and I was down with that. Everything about him turned me on. The way he talked, walked, and the way he said my name. This man was going to get it, and when he got it, I was giving him my all. Everyone would be like, *Aren't you Shaq's girl?* and I'd be like, *Shaq, who?* That nigga was going to be far from my mind.

Anyway, I was headed to drop Ken off at my mama's house. I could have let her take her, but I wanted an excuse to get out the house. Craig and I were supposed to meet up for dinner. After dropping Ken off at my mama's house, I headed to the mall to find something to throw on. Making it to the mall, I got out and headed to Forever 21. That was one of my favorite stores to shop at. Headed inside, I bumped into a cute Latina chick.

"Excuse me, my bad! I didn't see you," I told her honestly.

"I know you saw me, just watch where the hell you're going," she said with so much attitude. That wasn't a cute look on her.

"Damn, I said excuse me. What the hell is wrong with

you?" I asked, now in her face, ready to fight.

"Watch your back, because once I have this baby, I'm coming for you," she told me, walking off.

"Oh yeah, I'll be waiting," I yelled behind her. Her ass better come correct because I would light her ass up and not think twice.

These bitches these days were rude as fuck, but you better believe if I caught her again, I was tearing off in her ass. Making my way into Dillard's, I saw a bad-ass jumpsuit. Making my way over to it, I picked it up and held it close to my body. It was just right; it looked like it would fit me perfectly. It was a black, off the shoulder jumpsuit. It wasn't something I usually wore, but today wasn't a regular date. All I needed now was a pair of bad-ass heels.

Heading to the register, I paid for my stuff and headed to Citi Trends to find some heels to go with my outfit. Going inside Citi Trends, I headed to the heels section. They always had cute heels. Picking up a pair of silver heels that strapped around the ankles, I tried them on and walked over to the mirror. I loved how I looked in them. Deciding to find some accessories to go with everything, it took me no time to find some nice things. I was in and out of Citi Trends in no time. Making my way to the car, I heard my cell phone ringing, but I couldn't answer it because I had a hand full of bags. When I got to the car, I threw the bags in the trunk and checked my cell phone to see that Craig had called me. Dialing him back, he picked up on the first ring.

"Damn, I see you curving me already." He sounded so sexy on the other end. The way he said it had my kitty purring.

"My bad, baby, I was shopping. You know I gotta look sexy for you tonight."

"Baby, you know you can wear a trash bag, and you'll still look sexy." He knew what to say to make me blush.

I blushed and clenched my legs. "Awwww, baby, you are so sweet. Thank you."

"You know you're welcome, baby. I'll meet you at the restaurant tonight at eight, and make sure you leave the panties home." I swear his ass did the most.

"OK, baby, I'll see you later." I hung up the phone.

Heading back to my mother's house, I decided to call Shaq and let him know that I was staying over Mama's hose tonight. Dialing his number, he answered on the fourth ring.

"Yo, what's up, baby? Y'all on the way home?" he asked in a sleepy voice.

"About that. Me and Ken staying at Mama's house tonight. We'll be home first thing in the morning."

"OK, cool. Kiss my daughter for me," he said that a little too calmly, so I knew he was up to some shit.

"OK, baby, I'll talk to you later." I hung up before he could say I love you. I loved Shaq, but I wasn't in love with him. That had left a long time ago.

Sitting in my mother's driveway a little longer, I got out and got my stuff out the trunk. Making my way to the front door, I stuck my key in the hole to let myself in. Ken and my mama were sitting in the living room, watching *SpongeBob SquarePants*. Ken loved SpongeBob. Walking over to them, I picked Ken up and kissed her on the cheek.

"Hey, mama. I hope you don't mind watching Ken tonight. A friend and I are going out to catch up," I told her, walking over to her and kissing her on the cheek. She gave me the side-eye, and I knew she was about to start.

"A friend, huh?" She got up off the couch and headed to the kitchen.

"Yes, a friend, mama. That's all we are." My mother wasn't a fool, and she knew what was up.

"You know I don't mind watching my grandchild, but Monica, before you open another door, close the first one first," she told me. I knew she was about to start, but that was what I loved about her: she didn't believe in cheating. She always told me if it was meant to be, it would be.

"Mama, it's not even like that. We are just friends, that's it."

"OK, but remember what I told you." She held her hands up and walked out the kitchen.

Giving Ken back to my mama, I headed upstairs to my room that I had here. I decided to shower and get myself together. Turning the water on, I waited for it to get hot. Brushing my teeth and washing my face, I stripped out of my clothes and entered the shower. Grabbing my loofah, I squeezed some of my Dove body wash on it, making sure I got every inch of my body clean. Then, I quickly rinsed off and got out. Turning the water off, I grabbed my towel and dried off. Plugging up my flat iron, I went to my room and put on a matching bra and thong set. Sitting on the edge of the bed, I lotioned my body. Once I was satisfied, I walked back to the bathroom. Flat ironing my hair, I made sure I slicked my edges down. Once I was done, I looked like a million bucks. I didn't need makeup because my skin was flawless the way it was. Applying a little lip gloss, I blew myself an air kiss. Going back inside my room, I got dressed. Once I was done, I looked at the time, and it was a little after seven. Making my way to Ken's room, I peeked in and checked on her, and she looked like she was sleeping so peacefully. Walking over to her bed, I bent down and kissed her on the cheek. Making my way out of her room, I made sure I left her door cracked.

"OK, mama, I shouldn't be out long. I love you." I walked over to the couch and kissed her on the cheek.

"Baby, be careful. You are my only child, and I don't want anything to happen to you," she told me, standing up and kissing me on the forehead. I knew she was worried about me, but I was going to be careful.

"Mama, don't worry. I'm always careful. I'll call you and let you know I made it."

"OK, baby, enjoy yourself and don't worry about Ken. I got her," she told me as I was leaving out the door.

Making it to the car, I sent Craig a message to let him know I was on my way. Throwing my phone in the passenger seat, I started my car. Heading over to LongHorn, my stomach started turning. I didn't know if something was about to happen, or if it was something I had eaten earlier. It could have been that I was nervous because I knew tonight, it was going down. The ride over to LongHorn was quiet and quick. When I made it to LongHorn, Craig was out front, waiting for me. Finding a parking spot, I parked and was about to open the door, but Craig ran over and got it for me. He was so sweet.

"Thank you, baby. You are looking and smelling good," I told him, leaning into a hug. It was something about this man that made me weak in my knees.

"Anything for you, baby. Damn, you look good as fuck. I told you not to wear no panties, though. You hardheaded as fuck," he whispered in my ear. The way he whispered in my ear sent chills down my spine.

Grabbing his hand, we made our way inside. Once we got inside, it was busy as hell, so I was glad he had made a reservation because we would be waiting all night. Giving the waiter our names, we were seated.

"My name is Hailey, and I'll be your waitress tonight. Can I start you guys off with something to drink?"

"Yes, give me a glass of water with lemon," I told her.

"Give me a Bud light and a glass of water," Craig told her.

Once we placed our drink orders, she walked off. Craig looked like a whole snack on the other side of the booth. Damn, how could he be so damn fine and not have a woman? Hailey brought our drinks back, and I took a sip.

"So, Craig, why are you single?" I got straight to the point. No need to beat around the bush.

"Shit, I don't know. I'm a busy man, so I don't have time for a relationship. Hell, I hardly have time for myself. I usually just hit and keep it moving," he told me without blinking.

"So, I'm just a fuck to you, huh?" I asked, frowning with my arms folded across my chest. I was glad Craig was honest with me, though.

"Naw, it's not like that, ma. I see more in you. If you were just a fuck to me, I would have taken your ass to McDonald's and got a cheap hotel. I see something in you, and I wanna see how things go with us." He pulled my hands down and caressed them while looking into my eyes.

Once we placed our food order, I felt someone burning a hole in my back. Turning around slowly, my eyes met Shaq's, and I saw fire in his eyes. Damn, that was why my stomach had felt like that on the way over here. How could I get myself in this shit?

"Excuse me, baby, I need to go to the restroom." "Don't take too long. If you do, I might have to come get you," he told me as he winked at me. This man was everything I wanted in a man.

As I headed to the bathroom, I saw Shaq get up and follow me.

"So, this is why you wanted to stay with your mama? So you can be a hoe? Where the fuck is my child?" he spat as soon as we reached the bathroom.

"If you must know, Ken is with my mother, and I'm tired of your shit. So, yes, this is why I said I was staying with my mama," I told him with just as much attitude. He could get the hell out of my face with this bullshit. Hell, he was out fucking bitches, so why couldn't I do me?

"Dinner is over, so get your shit and let's ride." He grabbed my arm and squeezed a little too hard.

"I would let her go if I was you. You already got a death certificate, so unless you wanna meet your maker now, let her the fuck go." Craig was standing there with his gun aimed at Shaq. We were in a restaurant, but he didn't give a damn.

This nigga had a death sentence? What the fuck am I missing? Who had this nigga pissed off? What the fuck have I gotten myself into?

Letting me go, I ran into the bathroom to get myself together. This nigga had some nerve to bring his ass up in here, giving orders.

****

I decided to back off from Craig and get my shit together. The look in Shaq's eyes at the restaurant was scary. I knew I should have listened to what mother had said, and maybe I wouldn't have been in this situation. I thought I had been covering my tracks; I didn't know that Shaq was going to come looking for me. Now I was sitting here, thinking of how we could leave without Shaq knowing. Maybe we could leave while he was asleep, but who was I kidding? Shaq would only find us. I missed the hell out of Craig, but I knew we couldn't be. I laid in bed, thinking about him when Shaq walked into the room.

"What made you think I wasn't gonna come looking for you? When you called me, I knew you were up to no good. For you to leave my daughter with your mom so you could go out to be a hoe was the wrong move." Shaq kept going on and on, but I wasn't in the mood for his shit.

"Please get the hell out my face. I am not in the mood for your shit right now. We can pick this up later, but right now, I'm going to sleep."

"Naw, we gonna finish this now. Once I get whatever I need to say out, then you can take your ass to sleep." This time, I sat up and was all ears.

"Say what the fuck you gotta say, and after you finish, I'll say what I have to say. After that, I wanna take my ass to sleep. I just told your ass I was tired." I was so over this shit.

"I just want to know why you can't be happy with a nigga. I am done running behind Summer, and I just want us to be happy. We have our little family, and maybe we can add to it." This nigga had lost his damn mind. When I wanted him to love me, it was fuck me. Now, it was fuck him.

"Oh, so now you want to do right since Summer doesn't want your ass. You either get your shit together, or Ken and I are gone. I took too much of your shit as it is. Then you are so damn controlling. We used to go out, but that stopped. When you are here, it's like you aren't here. Shaq, I'm so tired of this shit. I was a fool before, but just know I won't be a fool again. If you can't keep your dick in your pants, just let me go." As I finished talking, the tears started streaming down my face. This nigga had humiliated me a time too many.

"Baby, I'm sorry. I am. I promise I'm gonna do right by you and Ken. We are gonna be a family. If I see that I want to step out on you, I will let you go." He walked over to me and held me. He sounded sincere, but I knew Shaq. His ass would do good for a week, and then he would be back to his whorish ways. I wasn't going to get my hopes up only to get my feelings hurt. We would see where this went, but one slip-up and I was done.

Chapter 7

Summer

Today was finally release day, and boy was I glad. Everybody here was so kind and caring, but there was nothing like sleeping in your own bed. I was waiting for them to release me and waiting for Troy to come back. While I was in the hospital, Troy had been nothing less than amazing. Even when he left me, if I called him, he always answered. Speaking of Troy, he was calling me right now.

"Hey, baby!" I wasted no time picking up. I couldn't take the stupid smile off my face.

"Hey, babe. I'm handling some stuff at the shop, but I should be there shortly. Is there anything you need while I'm out?"

"No, baby, I'm good, just hurry up. They should be releasing me shortly."

"OK, baby, let me finish up here, and I'm on my way. How are my babies doing? Put the phone on your stomach, I wanna talk to them." He always asked about his kids.

Placing the phone on my stomach, he started talking. I thought it was so cute. The kids were having a field day. I didn't know what he was saying, but they were going crazy. I heard him pressing keys, so I took the phone from my stomach and placed it back to my ear.

"What did you say to them? They are going crazy in here." I heard him laugh.

"Damn, you nosy. But naw, I told them to take care of each other, and give you hell while I'm gone." Now it was my turn to laugh; he was so damn silly.

"I love you, baby. I'll see you shortly."

"I love you, too, baby, and I'll be there shortly," he told me just before he hung up.

I was sitting on the bed, just thinking about my life and how I had gotten a second chance. I was never really into church, but when I got out of here, I would be going to church. I knew the Lord heard me, but there was nothing like being in the house of God.

Carla hadn't called me today, so I decided to call her and see how she was doing. When she first came to the hospital, she told me that she couldn't take seeing me like that. I knew she was taking it hard, but I needed her right now. Dialing her number, she picked up on the first ring.

"Hey, girl, how are you feeling today? I know I haven't been up to see you, but I'm going through something right now." I could tell by the tone of her voice that something was bothering her.

"What's wrong, boo? It's OK, I'm going home today anyway. Maybe you can come over and keep me company while Troy is at work."

"Girl, yes. Don't worry, I'll be over there a little later. Anyway, Sam and I are going through a little rough patch. He has been acting funny lately, and I'm about to lose my damn mind, girl." I could hear the hurt with every word she said.

"Carla, you might be taking things the wrong way. Have you talked to him about how you feel?" I was now concerned because I knew she was feeling Sam but was scared to open up to him.

"Yes, I have tried to call him, but when we talk, he keeps it short with me. I know Sam, and he has never acted like this with me. Maybe I should have waited a little longer to give up the goods," she laughed.

"Girl, now you know Sam worships the ground you walk on. Maybe y'all need to sit down so you can lay it all on the table." Recently, Carla had told me about her past and was scared to tell Sam because she thought he would leave her. Sam was a good man, and I didn't think he would leave her because of that.

"You right, girl. That's why you are my bestie. You know what to say to cheer me up. As soon as you get home, call me, and I'll be right over. Let me call Sam and see if he can meet me for lunch so I can get this over with."

"OK, boo, let me know how everything goes. You know I love you."

"I love you, too, boo. I'll see you later." She hung up, and I set my phone down on the table.

I was just about to call the nurse, and in walked the nurse with some paperwork, but it wasn't the same one who had been caring for me since I'd been here. She looked so familiar, though. Staring at her, she looked like someone I had gone to school with.

"Melinda, is that you?" Her eyes lit up, so I knew that's who it was.

"Summer, girl, it's been what, eight years since we've seen each other."

"Yes, it's me, fat and pregnant," I laughed.

"Congrats on your babies. I'm so happy for you." She walked over and hugged me. We were never close, but she was a good person.

"Thank you. I hope those are my discharge papers because I am so ready to go," I told her, laughing. Hell, I wasn't lying. I wanted a nice bubble bath and a nap. I couldn't sleep how I wanted to here.

"Yes, ma'am. We got you all squared away here. Your discharge papers tell you what you can and can't do, and we have an appointment set up for you next week at your OB/GYN office. Do you have any questions for me?" She handed me the paperwork.

"Nope, not at all. You have explained everything I need to know."

"Alrighty, sign right here, and you are free to go." She handed me the pen, and I scribbled my name down. I was finally free after a week.

Just as I was finishing signing the papers, Troy's sexy ass walked in. "Hey, baby, you all ready to go?" He walked over and bent down to kiss my lips, then he rubbed my stomach, and the kids started having a field day.

"Y'all calm down in there. Yes, we are ready to go," I told him, laughing.

"Thank you, Melinda, and I hope you have a good day," I told her as Troy wheeled me out of the room.

When I made it to the door, I inhaled some of the fresh air. I was so happy to be going home. I was not for sure if we would be staying at my apartment or if Troy had gotten us another place. Making our way to the car, Troy helped me into the passenger side. Before long, we would need a bigger ride because this Challenger wouldn't be big enough when the babies got here. Once I was in, Troy shut my door and headed to the driver's side.

"Baby, are y'all hungry?" Troy asked just before he pulled off.

"Not starving, but we can eat," I told him, rubbing my belly.

"OK, what you want? The usual?" he asked, laughing. He knew damn well these kids were picky as hell, so I didn't see why he had even asked. I just nodded.

Pulling off from the hospital, we were headed to Gina's Soul Food. I swear they had the best fried chicken. It was not as good as Mama's, but it was damn sure close. As soon as we pulled up, I wasn't going to get out until I saw Erica's ass. I looked over at Troy, and he shook his head. I wasn't about to show my ass unless she started it, so this hoe better stay in her lane.

"I don't know why the hell you shaking your damn head for," I told him with so much attitude. I also made it known numerous times that I didn't like the Erica chick. Hell, she could be pregnant by his ass, too.

"Man, don't start all that jealousy shit; it's not a good look on you, ma." He leaned over and kissed me. One peck led to a steamy make-out session, and I had to pull away before I said fuck this food and we ended up in the back seat.

"Troy, come on, we are hungry," I whined.

"Shit, I have my dinner right here, I don't need no damn food." He winked at me. This man turned me on in the worst way. I was soaking wet and had to squeeze my legs together. I was going to put it on him once we got to the house.

Getting out the car, he came to my side and opened the

door for me. Grabbing his hand, he led me into the restaurant. Inside, it wasn't that busy, and I was glad because I was now starving. Looking to my right, I decided to be petty and wave at Erica. If looks could kill, I would be one dead bitch. She made it known that she wasn't fucking with me, but the feeling was mutual. Finding a booth on the opposite side, I slid in and waited for Troy to come back. Just as I was pulling out my cell phone, Erica's ass wobbled up to Troy, so I got my fat ass out the booth and wobbled my ass over there, too.

"Troy, me and your baby need you, too. Her kids are not the only kids you have." She pointed at me.

"Erica, until you give me a DNA test, these are the only kids I have." He pointed at me, and I must say, Troy had put her ass in her place.

"You win. I'll make an appointment at my OB to set it up. Once I get a date and time, I will call you with it."

"No, hoe, you won't call him. Call my phone, and I will relay the message. Until we know that this baby is Troy's, he won't be doing a damn thing for it," I told her with so much attitude. I didn't give a damn though because she wasn't about to pin a child on my man. Fuck all that.

"Listen here, you little bitch. I wasn't talking to your fat ass. This has nothing to do with you. I didn't lay down and fuck you, so if you know what's best for you, you will stay the hell out of this." This hoe called herself going off on me, but she better sit her Kim Kardashian wannabe ass down somewhere.

"Listen here, you little bitch, this has everything to do with me. Troy is my man, so like I said, when you have the date and time, call me, and I'll tell him. Trust me, you don't want these problems, boo." I was now in her face, and from the way she was breathing, I could tell she was mad. I didn't give a damn though because she had the right one. Troy stepped in between us.

"Summer, baby, I got this. Go ahead and sit down. Our food should be ready shortly." Troy kissed me on the lips, and I went back over to the booth to sit down. This woman had pissed my babies of too because they were kicking the hell out of me.

"Calm down, mama's babies. I'm sorry, but she made me step out of my character," I said while rubbing my stomach.

About five minutes later, Troy came walking over to the table with our food. As soon as he placed my plate in front of me, I went to work. I was so damn hungry by now, I inhaled the food. Finishing my food, I watched Troy eat. While watching him, I felt a phone vibrate. Looking down at my phone, I noticed it wasn't mine. Putting down his fork, Troy retrieved his phone from his pocket.

"Give me a minute, baby, I need to take this." He got up from the table and headed outside.

From the way he looked, I knew it was a heated conversation. He might not tell me now, but I knew once he calmed down, he was going to tell me about the conversation. A little while later, Erica headed out the door.

"Bye, girl, we will talk soon." I was still being messy.

"I guess." She threw her hand up and waved. I was glad she had seen it my way. If she stayed in her lane, we wouldn't have any problems.

At seven months pregnant, I was using the bathroom more, so getting up from the booth, I made my way into the bathroom. Once I relieved my bladder, I made my way to the sink and washed my hands. Looking in the mirror, I saw that I was big as hell. I looked like a big-ass whale, but I was still sexy. Washing my hands, I headed back to the booth and Troy was standing there, waiting for me.

"Sorry about that, baby. You ready to go?" He walked up to me and grabbed my hand.

"Yes, baby, I'm tired as hell. All I want to do is lay down," I told him honestly. Hell, who was I kidding? As soon as I got in the car, I was going to be out.

Heading out the restaurant, Troy opened my door, and I slid in. Closing my door, he jogged around to the driver's side and got in. Starting the car, we headed home, but I noticed Troy had passed the road to my apartment.

"Bae, you missed the road to the apartment. Where are we going?"

"As I told you before we got into that accident, you will never stay another night in that apartment."

"I need my clothes and some other stuff out of the apartment," I told him in one breath.

"Calm down, baby. I had some of my people go over there and pack everything up. They took it to our new place." He smiled at me.

"I swear I love the hell out of you, Troy. If you ever think you are leaving us, you can think again. I will kill you if I have to." I was dead ass serious. Troy was it for me. I had been through enough shit in my life.

"Damn, baby, you'll kill a nigga?" he asked, laughing.

"If you only knew what I would do to you. We are in a good space right now, so let's stay that way."

We talked until we made it to our new place. When Troy pulled into the driveway, I was lost for words. The house was big and pretty, a light gray color, and the lawn looked like it had been freshly cut. I felt the tears falling from my eyes. I was an emotional wreck.

"Baby, what are you crying for?" Troy wiped the tears from my eyes.

"This house is beautiful. If the front yard is this big, I can imagine what the back looks like. Thank you so much, baby." I damn near jumped across the seat to hug him.

"No thanks needed, baby. This is for our little family. We will raise our kids here. Come on, let me show you the inside."

Opening my door, I wobbled my ass up to the front door. The more I walked, the harder I breathed. I was so ready to have my body back. Just as I was making it up the steps, Troy walked up behind me and opened the door. When I entered the house, it was breathtaking. The carpet was white and fluffy. I took off my shoes and walked on it, and it felt like I was walking on clouds. The living room was fully furnished, and whoever decorated had great taste. I sat on the couch and laid my head back.

"Baby, how did you manage to get all of this setup? This is beautiful," I told him with my eyes closed. He just didn't know, but we were about to take a nap right here.

"I'm glad you like it. It wasn't easy, but I'll do anything for y'all. I know you are about to go to sleep, so when you get up, I'll show you the rest of the house." He came and kissed my forehead.

"Thank you, baby. I love you." I closed my eyes again and tried to relax. When I couldn't get comfortable, I got up and called Carla. While I was waiting for her to answer, I went to the kitchen and got something to drink.

"Hey, girl, you home? I just left your place, and it was empty. Where the hell are you?" If she gave me a chance to explain, I would tell her exactly where I was.

"Sis, you won't believe me if I told you, but I'm about to text you an address. When you get to the address, let me know. Hurry up!" I told her just before I hung up. I knew she was going to get in my ass when she got here, but we would cross that bridge when she got here.

I had not too long ago texted her the address, and she had texted me, telling me she was outside. I got up from the chair and made it to the door, and Carla was sitting in the car, looking crazy. I had to laugh at her stupid ass. Waving her over, she got out the car and made it to the door. She gave me a sisterly hug and rubbed my belly. I moved out the way and let her inside. She looked around like she had never seen anything like this. I knew she was about to start.

"Can I get you something to drink or eat?" I was trying to show my manners.

"Bitch, no, I'm good! I ate not too long ago. Whose house is this?" This hoe didn't give me a chance to sit down before she was firing off questions.

"If you must know, this is mine and Troy's house. While I was in the hospital, Troy got this for us. I knew his ass was up to some shit, but I didn't think he was going to get us a house. When we left the hospital, I thought we were going to my apartment, but when we passed my road, I knew some shit was up. As soon as we pulled up, my ass started boo-hoo crying. I wasn't sure whose house it was, but I assumed it was ours." Carla was on the other couch, dying laughing.

"I swear I can't wait for you to have my niece and nephew. All your ass do is cry. You can be watching SpongeBob, and your ass starts crying. That shit is not a good look for you, with your crybaby ass." She did the most, but I had to laugh because she was right.

"Shut up, I can't help that I am the way I am. For real, though, I can't wait to have them, either. I look like a big whale. My feet are always swollen, and every way I try to sleep, I can't get comfortable. I am so over this damn pregnancy. If someone had told me it was like this, I would have kept my damn legs shut." Troy wouldn't catch me slipping anymore.

"Sis, you are big as hell, but you are cute with it, though. At least you don't look like some of these sloppy bitches out here. We gonna have to work extra hard because you done gained what, 100 pounds?" She looked at me and laughed. Hell, I was knocking on 100 pounds. I had gained ninety-four pounds and was still growing.

"Bitch, I'm close to it. You don't have to keep reminding me that I'm fat. I can look in the mirror and see that. That's OK though because as soon as my six weeks are up, I will be in somebody's gym. I can't keep this weight on me. I know Troy will love me no matter what, but I can't see me like this." I got up and pointed to my body.

"Girl, please, you are all baby. That weight will fall off once you have them. Have y'all come up with their names yet?"

"Nope, we are waiting for them to get here, then we will name them. I know Troy wants a Jr., and I'm cool with that, and I want the girl to have my mother's middle name. I miss her so much." Talking about my mother always made me emotional, so that was why I tried not to talk about her.

"I know, boo. I miss her, too. I know she is proud of you, though, and she's probably smiling down on you now." She walked over to where I was sitting and hugged me. I was so glad I had her to talk to. When Troy wasn't home, I knew she was going to be over here.

We talked for a little longer, and she told me she had to go. I wasn't ready for her to leave just yet, and I didn't want to call and worry Troy because I knew he was out handling business. We said our goodbyes, and just that quickly, I started missing Troy. Locking the door, I went into the kitchen and got something to eat. Troy made sure I had a lot of fruit and water in the house. He told me he wanted his kids to come out healthy. I understood where he was coming from, though. He had been the best thing that had happened to my life, except when I found out I was pregnant with twins. Grabbing an apple and a bottle of water, I headed back into the living room. Turning the TV on, as I expected, there was nothing on. I turned it off and finished my snack. Deciding to try taking a nap, I got as comfortable as I could on the couch, and just like that, I was out for the count.

Chapter 8

Troy

While Summer and I were out enjoying lunch, my nigga Craig had called me. At first, I wasn't going to answer, but I felt it was something important. I excused myself from the booth and made my way outside.

"Yeah, tell me something good," I answered.

"Man, why can't I kill this nigga? He all in my way. Tell me why we're fucking with the same woman. When I was sitting outside of his crib, and she walked out, I wanted to go in and blow his damn brains out. His ass is so damn disrespectful." I could tell he was mad as shit.

"Calm down, killer. The time is coming, and once the time is right, I'll let you help torture him," I told him.

"When is the time gonna be right? I'm telling you, if he put his hands on baby girl again, I'ma have to kill his ass. I'm starting to feel little mama more." The way he said it, I knew he was serious, too.

"Just hold off a little while longer. I gotta make sure my baby is good, and I'll link up with you later," I told him just before hanging up with him.

"See you later, baby daddy," Erica threw over her shoulder as she headed to her car. I didn't feel a connection with this baby like I did with my other two.

When I looked at the restaurant, Summer looked tired as shit, so I had to get my baby home so she could lay down. Making my way back inside, I asked if she was ready to go. Telling me that she was, we made our way to the car. Making sure Summer was in the car, I closed the door and headed to my side. Driving to the house, we made small talk. I knew Summer was going to ask where we were going, but I told her once we weren't going to spend another day in that apartment. I wanted something our kids could grow up in. Plus, since that nigga was still paying for that apartment, it was a no-go in my book. I didn't want anything from that nigga. I had a slow death for him, though. It was too easy to put a bullet through his skull, I wanted more. He had almost killed my baby and our kids.

Pulling up to our new house, Summer's ass started boo-hoo crying like someone had taken the last piece of pie. This pregnancy was taking a toll on her, and I saw it. She just didn't know that once she had my first two kids, she was going to be pregnant again. She knew I wanted a house full of kids. The way her ass looked in that dress had my dick harder than a rock. I had business to handle, though, and I knew she was tired. Heading in the house, she laid on the couch, and I knew she was about to be out.

"Baby, I'll be back a little later. The kitchen is stocked if you get hungry. Call me if you need anything while I'm out," I told her, kissing her on the forehead.

Making sure I locked the house up on the way out, I let the garage up and took my car out. I needed to put Summer's car in the garage, but I'd do it as soon as I got back. Pulling out my cell, I dialed Sam up, and he picked up on the first ring.

"Damn, nigga, let the phone ring," I joked with him.

"Man, nigga, fuck you. I was waiting for Carla to call. She texted me talking about we needed to talk," he said, frustrated as hell.

"Well, we got business to handle. I'll be over to pick you up in a minute," I told him, hanging up the phone.

I needed to get with Carla, too. I needed her help picking out a ring for Summer since she was the closest thing to family Summer had. I was about to give my baby the world. Pulling out the driveway, I headed to pick up Sam. When I pulled up to his crib, he looked stressed out. Opening the passenger side door, he got in.

"Damn, nigga, you good? You look like you haven't slept in days." I laughed at his ass.

"Yeah, man, I'm good, but Carla is stressing me the fuck out, man. How 'bout she called me and told me she thought we needed space. Carla gonna make me jack her little ass up. She is a happy place for me, and she wanna take that away from me," he told me with a pissed off look on his face.

"Give her time, she will come around. Little Sis loves yo' ass." I wasn't lying.

"Fuck that, we can work this shit out together. It ain't no way I'ma give her ass no space. Fuck you mean?"

"Calm down, my nigga, I'm just saying. Anyway, we 'bout to meet Craig and discuss business. Come to find out, Craig is involved with his ol' lady."

"No way, man. Damn, it's a small world. Where the hell we meeting at? A nigga is hungry as fuck."

"You look hungry as fuck, too. Look like you haven't eaten in days." I cracked a joke on his ass. Love was crazy, though, so I knew exactly what he was going through.

Pulling up to Buffalo Wild Wings, I saw Craig's truck, and I knew his ass was already eating. Sam and I got out and headed inside. As I thought, Craig was at the bar, eating some wings. Walking up to him, he wiped his hands off and stood up to dap us up.

"What's good, my brother? I see you started the party without us." I gave him a brotherly hug.

"Hell yeah, y'all niggas were taking too long. A nigga was hungry as hell," Craig's goofy ass started.

"So, let's get down to business. Craig, what you got for me?" I sat down, and I was all ears.

"All I gotta say is that nigga got to go; he put his hands on someone close to me." I saw the smoke coming from his ears, and I knew for a fact if we didn't do something quick, Craig would indeed kill this nigga.

"Chill, bro, we gonna get that nigga. I got plans to torture his ass, then we will send a body part a day to his mama. Hell, better yet, we can ship the whole body to her door." This nigga was indeed getting what was coming to him.

"Can we just get this shit over with? I need to meet up with Carla and give her some act right. Talking 'bout damn space, she got me all the way fucked up. When she opened her legs for me, that sealed the deal." Sam was mad as hell, and his face turned red as a tomato.

"You know what, Craig, I'll be in touch. Let me get this nigga home before he loses his mind." I stood up and dapped Craig.

"Sam, you need to go change your pad, I can see the blood trying to leak through," Craig clowned Sam. This nigga was a straight fool.

"Fuck you, nigga. Get you some business," Sam spat as he walked out the restaurant. I couldn't do anything but shake my damn head. These two niggas had me rolling. When we got to the car, I popped the lock, and we got in. Sam slammed my door, and I gave that nigga the side-eye. "Nigga, don't be slamming my shit. Hell, it didn't do shit to your ass."

"My bad, man, a nigga just stressed out. I have never been this way with any woman. This shit is wild. I know Carla is something special to me." Sam now had a frown on his face.

"Nigga, if it's meant to be, she will come back to you. I can tell by how Carla looks at you that she loves your ass. Women are different from men, so give her time, man. She might be scared, so maybe that's why she is pulling away from you."

As Sam and I were having a heart to heart conversation, my phone rang. Looking down at it, I saw that it was Erica. I knew Summer had made it clear that she was to call her phone, and I wasn't about to get caught up in her shit. I let it go to voicemail, and once I got home, I would call her back. Summer and I were at a happy place, and I wasn't about to jeopardize it for her hoe ass. The crazy thing about it, though, my phone rang again, and it was her again. I knew something had to be up with her calling back to back like this. Deciding to answer the phone, I put it on speaker phone, so I could have a witness. I put my finger up to my mouth to silence Sam as I picked up.

"Yeah, man. Your ass better be in labor or some shit because I know we made it clear that you aren't supposed to call a nigga." I was trying to be nice to her hoe ass.

"Nigga, I tried to call Summer before I called you and Summer is in trouble. You need to get to her." When she said Summer was in trouble, it was like my world stopped. I swear I was going to kill this nigga with my bare hands.

I hung up the phone and sped to my house. Sam's ass

would have to roll with me until I made sure my baby was OK. I didn't care, I was running stop signs, red lights and all. If them boys got behind me, they would have to follow me to my house because I wasn't stopping. It took me a little over twenty minutes to get to the house, and I didn't even remember putting the car in park before I jumped out with Sam in tow.

Getting to the door, it looked like someone had kicked it in. Running in the house, I yelled for Summer, but it was too quiet. I sent a silent prayer to the Man upstairs before pulling out my burner and running upstairs. Taking two steps at a time, something felt off. When I made it to our bedroom, I pushed the door open, and the sight in front of me had me seeing red. There was a big-ass nigga on my baby, raping her. Her legs and arms were tied up, and they had the nerve to have a sock stuffed in her mouth. Clicking the safety off my gun, I shot the nigga in the back of his head, and he fell off Summer. Running over to her, I untied her. Sam was right there and made sure that nigga was dead by sending two more bullets through his head.

When I untied her, she fell into my arms, crying, and that shit tugged at a nigga's heart. One thing I vowed to her was to always protect her, and I had failed at that. A nigga had murder on his mind. Something told me Shaq was behind this shit, but I wasn't for sure.

"Sssshhhh, baby, I got you. I'm sorry I wasn't here for you when you needed me. Don't worry, I will never leave your side again." Damn man, I felt like a failure.

"Baby, I was so scared, and you weren't here for me," she cried harder.

"Baby, I'm sorry. Come on, let's get you cleaned up so I can take you to the hospital. We need to make sure you and the babies are good."

Pulling her out the bed, I helped her to the bathroom. As we were walking to the bathroom, I heard a loud gushing sound. As I looked down, it looked like Summer was pissing on herself. I knew this couldn't be happening. Summer's water had just broken. It was a little early for her to go into labor, so I instantly froze up.

"Oh my God, baby, my water just broke! We need to get to the hospital!" she yelled.

Running in the bathroom, I got a washcloth and cleaned Summer up. When we made it out the bathroom, that bitch-made nigga had been removed from the floor. I knew Sam had called the clean-up crew to get his ass. I didn't give a damn what they did with him. Putting on her clothes, we headed out the room, and I had forgotten all about Sam being there until we made it downstairs to the living room. Sam stood up and looked like he was ready to go.

"I heard Sis scream, so I can drive y'all there. Come on, y'all, I don't want my niece and nephew born here. Although this is a nice crib, I think we need to be where they can get the help they need." Sam sounded so sincere.

Once I made sure Summer was in the car and was as comfortable as possible, I ran back up to the house and pulled the door up. I knew I needed to get someone to fix the door. Making it back to the car, I got in, and Sam peeled off. Sam was driving like a bat out of hell. It didn't matter, though, as long as we got my baby to the hospital. Looking over at her, she was trying to keep her breathing under control.

"Oh, shit, please hurry the hell up! I feel like I gotta push!" Summer screamed, and that made Sam speed up.

When we finally made it to the hospital, we pulled up to the emergency room area. Running inside, I got a wheelchair so I could get Summer out the car. Once she sat down, I pushed her through the door. Once inside, I walked up to the lady at the desk. "Excuse me, ma'am, my girlfriend is in labor. Can we get some help?" I was trying to be as calm as possible, but I felt myself about to nut up.

"Pull a number, and we will be with you shortly." Her ignorant ass was smacking on gum while on the phone. I counted to three in my head, but that didn't calm me down one bit.

"Listen, you little bitch, I told your ratchet ass that my girlfriend is in labor, so I ain't pulling no damn number. Get us some help, or I'll blow your brains out." I pulled my burner out on her ass. I was done playing with this bitch.

"Troy, the babies are coming, and I can't hold them in. What is going on?" Summer yelled.

"Bruh, calm yo' ass down. I don't need to bail you out of jail. Summer and the babies need you." What Sam said calmed me down.

"Baby, hold on, they are getting somebody for us," I told her as I kissed her lips.

"Oh my, God, I hate you, Troy!" I knew she'd had another contraction.

Five minutes later, they were wheeling us back to the room. The doctor she had been seeing was out of the country on vacation, so the doctor on call had to deliver the babies. When a tall, old, white man walked in, I looked at Sam, and he gave me a look like, *calm down, nigga.*

"My name is Dr. Holmes, and I will be delivering the

babies today. I would like to check and see how far you have dilated."

Walking over to the sink, he washed his hands and put a pair of gloves on. He walked over to where Summer was on the bed. "OK, I need you to open your legs so I can check."

Summer opened her legs, and I could see one of the baby's head. "OK, so one of the babies is at the opening, so we don't have time. We need to move," Dr. Holmes stated calmly.

I stood behind him, and it felt like I was about to pass out. Going over to the sink, I splashed some water on my face. All of this was a little too much for me, but I wouldn't miss it for anything in the world. Suiting up, I was ready to help bring my kids into the world. I was tired of all the mood swings. I was tired of it all, but I would do it all over again if it were with Summer.

"OK, give me one good push, and Baby A will be out," Dr. Holmes stated calmly. This nigga must have done this a lot because this shit didn't faze him. He was a little too close to Summer's pussy, though. Nigga was about to make me show my ass in here.

Taking a deep breath, Summer pushed, and out came the baby. I instantly fell in love all over again. He had the prettiest set of eyes, and a head full of curly hair, but he wasn't crying, so I instantly panicked. The nurses took him and cleaned him up, then she spanked him on the butt, and out came the cries. He had a set of lungs on him. He was five pounds, three ounces, and twenty-one inches long. He was beautiful. Heading back over to Summer, she looked exhausted. The machines started beeping, and I didn't know what was going on.

"The baby is in distress. We need to get her down to the

OR for an emergency C-Section. Move, guys," Dr. Holmes threw out orders. My baby was going in and out of consciousness, and I hoped like hell they could save both of my babies.

"I'm right here, baby. I ain't going nowhere. Stay with me, baby; we need you." Seeing her like this was fucking a nigga up, and I prayed they were safe.

Once we got in the OR, the nurses and doctors were running around, going crazy. They gave Summer an epidural, and everything went by fast. Next thing I knew, baby girl was out. She was small as shit, but she was beautiful no doubt. They told us she was breathing like she was supposed to, and as soon as we got a peek at her, they took her and started working on her. She was a fighter, so I knew she was going to make it out on top. Kissing Summer on her forehead, I walked over to make sure our baby was okay. When I got over there, the nurses were hooking her up to tubes. She had tubes in her nose to feed her, and to help her breath. Baby girl was four pounds, ten ounces, and twenty inches long. She was smaller than her brother, but I could tell she was going to be a problem. She had charcoal grey eyes, and she was a redbone, so I knew I had to keep my gun loaded.

"You did it, bae! You gave me my first kids, and I will always love you for that. We have to name them. What you got in mind?" I asked as I kissed her forehead.

"Troy Jamal Davis Jr. and Taylor Glory Davis." I liked the sound of that. She had given our daughter her mother's name, and I knew she was smiling down from heaven now. I saw a tear fall from her eye, and wiping her tears, I kissed her again.

"Get some rest, baby. I know you're tired, but I'm so glad

everything went well. I'ma let Sam and Carla know what's going on. I'ma also call Erica and thank her for calling me when she did." I kissed her on the forehead.

"Tell her I said thank you as well. I knew once she called me and heard everything that was going on, she would call you. I'm glad she did because if not, I probably would have died." She started crying. Now that she'd had the babies, she was still an emotional wreck. She was still shaken up, so I understood.

Kissing her one last time, I headed out the room to find Sam. When I found him, I saw that Carla was with him. Lil Sis was stressing my nigga out.

"Is my sister OK?" she asked in between sniffles.

"Yeah, sis, calm down. Summer had the babies. Jr was born vaginally, but Taylor had to be born via C-Section. Summer is resting right now, but you can check on her. She is in room 302." I couldn't get the room number out before she ran off. Gotta love Sis, though.

"Thanks, man, for having my back. Man, I don't know what I would have done if something would have happened to Summer," I told him honestly. Summer was my whole life.

"Bro, you know I got your back no matter what. It killed me to see that nigga on top of Summer like that. I wanted to bring that nigga back and kill him again." He was dead ass serious.

"I know, man, and I'ma find out who sent him, even though I feel like Shaq was behind it. You and Sis okay, though?"

"Yeah, man, we good. She just doesn't know she 'bout to be wifey." He was cheesing hard as hell.

We talked for a little while longer, and I had to get back to

Summer and my kids. It felt good being a father. Life was good.

Chapter 9

Summer

I had just gotten up from a much-needed nap, but I wasn't fully rested like I should have been. Wobbling upstairs, I finally made it to what I thought could be Troy and I's bedroom. The whole house was pretty as hell. When I walked into the bedroom, it was painted a cream color. I knew I had to put my touch on it, but it wasn't bad at all. In the middle of the room was a big bed made for a king and queen and I instantly fell in love with it. Walking over to the bed, I fell in it on my back. Lord, I needed to get my ass up and take a bath. Today had drained me. Going over to the dresser, I pulled out a bra and panty set. Stepping into the bathroom, I was lost for words; it was gorgeous. Turning the water on in the tub, I waited for it to fill up. Feeling a sharp pain rip through me, I knew it couldn't be time for these babies.

"Ah, please not now!" I said to myself. The pain wasn't severe, but it still hurt.

Deciding to go ahead and get in the tub to see if the pain would go away, I slipped in the tub, and laid there, the water relaxing my body. Dozing off, I woke up when I felt the water get cold. Standing up, I turned the shower on and washed my body a couple of times. Rinsing, I felt satisfied, so I got out. Grabbing a towel off the rack, I dried my body off. Stepping back in the room, I put my bra and panty set on. Falling onto the bed, I drifted off to sleep. I was awakened by another sharp pain, and this one was a little more intense.

Getting up, I made my way to the bathroom. Relieving my bladder, I got up and washed my hands. The pains were getting stronger and stronger. I thought about calling Troy, but I decided against it. I knew he would be back shortly. Making it back in the bedroom, I laid back down. I thought I heard someone downstairs, but figured it was Troy coming in. Kicking the bedroom door in, a male walked in. When I saw him, my body froze. What could this man possibly want with my pregnant ass? Once I snapped out of my daze, I grabbed my phone. I was just about to dial 9-1-1 when he grabbed my phone and threw it on the bed.

"No, please don't hurt me," I begged and pleaded with the male.

"Bitch, shut the fuck up. You can either give it to me, or I take it." He was in my face. To say I was scared was an understatement. I was frightened, not only for me but for my babies as well.

Throwing me on the bed, I felt helpless. This man was about to rape me, and I couldn't do anything about it. I tried to fight him off, but it was no use. He was stronger than me, and I couldn't stand up to him. He took some rope out and started tying my arm and leg to the bedpost, and I sat there and cried. Feeling my phone vibrate, I looked down, and it was Erica, so I quickly slid the bar over to answer it. Moving over the phone so he couldn't see it, I hoped like hell Erica called Troy before this man hurt us. Erica might just save our lives.

"Please, you can have anything you want, just don't hurt me," I pleaded with him.

"Little bitch, shut the fuck up. I'm about to sample this pussy, and there ain't shit you can do about it." He tugged at my underwear, and I sent a silent prayer up to the Man upstairs and laid there. There wasn't anything I could do.

He was eye level with pussy and started eating it. I didn't

want it to feel good, but it felt so damn good. I was sexually frustrated, so this was just what I needed. Feeling my orgasm rise, I busted a much-needed nut. I didn't want to, but since he was feasting, I might as well act like I enjoyed it. I felt a tear fall from my eye. He pulled his dick out and shoved it into my pussy. That shit hurt like hell. My cries fell on deaf ears because all he wanted to do was get his rocks off. While he was pumping in and out of me, I heard someone come inside the room. Looking up, I saw it was Troy and Sam. I felt so disgusted. I didn't want Sam to see me like this—he wasn't supposed to see me like this.

Seeing Troy pull out his gun and shoot him, I felt so relieved. If Troy hadn't come in when he did, this fucker would have gotten a good-ass nut. Troy made his way over to me, and I cried as he untied me. Troy was my safety net. I felt like nothing or no one would hurt me while he was around. Once he had me untied, I fell into his arms.

"Ssshhhh, baby, I got you. I'm sorry I wasn't there for you when you needed me, but I promise I will never leave your side again." Troy held me in his arms, rubbing my back.

"Baby, I was so scared," I cried harder. I wanted to be mad at him, but at the same time, I felt like it was my fault. If I had gone with him, all of this wouldn't have happened. I felt another sharp pain, and I flinched. I just hoped the babies weren't trying to make their debut; we weren't ready yet. Carla was supposed to throw me a baby shower this weekend, but I guess they had other plans.

"Baby, come on, let's get you cleaned up so I can get you to the hospital."

Slowly getting up off the bed, the pain was getting more intense. While heading to the bathroom, I felt something warm flow down my legs. I knew I was a bit early so this couldn't be happening. Whether I wanted it to or not, it was happening, and I couldn't stop it.

"Oh my God, baby, my water broke! We need to get to the hospital!" I yelled.

It hurt like hell, and I felt like I needed to push. Troy was running around like a chicken with his head chopped off, but he was doing the best he could, and I appreciated him. I panicked because I didn't want my babies to come at the house. I needed medical care.

"Come on, baby, let me clean you up so we can head to the hospital." Troy had a stranded look on his face.

Getting me to the bathroom, Troy helped me get cleaned up, and my mind was all over the place. I wanted to be mad at Troy, but at the end of the day, he had business to handle, and nobody knew any of this was going to happen. I had to be strong for our babies, though, and I prayed they were OK. Once Troy was done, he helped me put on my clothes, and we were out the door. Sam drove so Troy could ride in the back with me. I didn't know if I could take these pains again. It felt like someone was ripping my insides out.

Making it to the hospital, Troy went in to get help, and everything went so fast after they hooked me up to all the machines. Next thing I knew, I was giving birth to Jr. When the doctor told us baby girl was in distress, I blacked out. From my understanding, she was breech, and her heart rate kept dropping. Once they got her out, Taylor needed a little more help breathing, so they had all kinds of tubes in my baby's nose. I didn't know what I would do if my baby didn't make it. Troy told me he was heading out to tell Sam the good news, then he kissed me and was out the door. Laying my head back on the pillow, I tried to close my eyes and go to sleep. I was emotional, though, so sleep was the last thing I could do. Hearing the door open, I looked up and saw Carla. It looked like she had been crying, and I hope she didn't come in here with that. Rushing over to me, she squeezed me tight.

"I'm so sorry, sis. Sam told me what happened. I should have stayed over there until Troy came back. I'm sorry," she cried. I had told myself I wasn't going to cry anymore, but once I saw Carla crying, that was all over.

"Sis, it's not your fault. Don't beat yourself up about this. Trust and believe, Troy and Sam will take care of this." I sniffled and wiped the tears that were falling from my eyes.

"How are the babies? Troy told me you had them," Carla beamed.

"Troy is doing fine, but Taylor needed a little help breathing, so they have her hooked up to all kinds of machines. She's a fighter, so I know she will be fine," I told her.

"Can we go see them? I want to see my niece and nephew. I know they are cute as hell," Carla beamed.

"Yeah, let me call the nurse so they can wheel me down." I pushed the call button and asked the nurse to come get me so I could see my babies.

Wasting no time, the nurse came and got us, and we headed down to the nursey. Once we got there, Jr. was cutting up like I knew he would be. I knew he would be my problem child. Walking over to the sink, we washed our hands and went back over to the babies. Taylor was as cute as a button. She was tiny as hell, though. Carla was holding Jr. and talking to him, which made him calm down instantly. Sitting down in one of the rockers in the nursery, the nurse put Taylor in my arms, and my heart melted just looking at her. She had a head full of hair, and pretty, grey eyes.

"You need to fight, baby. Mama and Daddy need you," I whispered and felt the tear threatening to fall. I was trying to be strong for her, but I had failed as the tears started rolling down my face. I held her for a little while longer, then Carla came over and held her.

"She's so little, sis, but baby girl is a fighter. Look at her smiling at me. This is gonna be Auntie's baby." She kissed Tay's head.

We stayed with them for a little while longer, then we headed back to the room. Carla and I were talking, and the next thing I knew, Carla ran off after some ratchet-ass chick. Shaking my head, I knew it was Rhonda's ass. She had described her to the T. I just hoped Carla didn't do anything stupid to land her ass in jail. I knew Sam would get her out, but that was beside the point. When the nurse wheeled me to the room, I grabbed my phone and dialed Troy.

"Hey, baby, everything good?" He sounded so sincere.

"No, tell Sam to come down to my room and get Carla. I don't want her ass to land in jail."

"I'm on it, baby. I'll see you in a minute. I love you," he told me just before he hung up.

Sending a prayer up to the Man upstairs, I just hoped she didn't do anything stupid. Carla was too old to be out here showing out. I thought she would leave that to the younger generation, but she told me that every time she saw her, she was going to beat her ass. I knew she had tried to pin a baby on her man, but damn, she was doing too much. I felt sorry for Rhonda though because after the baby was born, she was going to indeed get her ass beat.

Two hours later

That little nap I had was just what I needed. I felt like I had slept for days. I guess having the babies drained me. As I looked to my left, Troy was laying beside me, sleeping so peacefully. I didn't know how he did it, though. This damn bed was so uncomfortable. I moved a little to get up out of bed, and the pain was unbearable. Troy shot up out the bed so damn quick, I had to laugh.

"Baby, you all right? What you need me to do for you?" He was cute, catering to my every need.

"I'm good, baby. I just want to get up and walk around, but I have no strength." I tried to get up again, and this time, I was successful. I walked to the door and back about three times. I was slow, but hey, that was a start.

"Don't overdo it, babe, you did just have babies. Take your time. You will be back at it before you know it." Troy was telling me some real shit, but I wasn't hearing it.

"I know, I'm good, baby, I'm just gonna walk one more time, and then I'm finished." I didn't want to get stiff, so I knew I had to keep my muscles moving.

When I made it back to the bed, Troy grabbed me and hugged me, and I melted into his embrace. I could stay like this all day. The event that had happened before the twins came into the world kept replaying in my head. I wanted this all to be over. Why couldn't I catch a break? I knew Troy felt me tense up, so I was going to ease the tension.

"So, since I had your babies, when can I get my push present?" Troy looked at me like I was crazy.

"What the hell is a push present? I haven't heard of no shit like that." I burst out laughing at his ass. His face was all balled up.

"A push present is something the partner gives to the mother of their child for giving birth. In this case, you owe me two push presents because I gave you two beautiful babies." I kissed him on his lips.

"You can get that, baby. Whatever you want, it's yours. At first, you had me confused as hell, but now I understand. What do you want for your push presents?" he asked just before he kissed my lips.

"Well, since you asked, I can use a bigger car. It doesn't have to be fancy, just something comfortable for the kids. The other one, it doesn't matter, just whatever you want to give me." He looked like he had something up his sleeve.

"You got it, baby. Once we get out of here, we can go look for something bigger. What about a minivan?"

"You tried it, baby. You won't catch me driving no minivan. Maybe a nice little truck, I'm good with that." I shrugged my shoulders.

"Cool, you got it. You ready to see the babies, though? Daddy misses his babies." It was like he could read my mind.

"Yeah, let's go." We got off the bed and walked to the nursery.

Chapter 10

Carla

"Didn't I tell you when I saw your ass I was gonna fuck you up?!" I slapped the shit out of Rhonda's stupid ass. I knew she was pregnant, but her face wasn't pregnant.

"All this over a man I once had. I know one thing's for certain, he will be back." She spat on my foot. This bitch had to be crazy. There was no way in hell Sam was going back to her.

I started to charge at her again, and I felt a strong pair of arms grab me by the waist. I knew it was Sam because of the cologne he wore. Versace Eros was now my favorite scent for Sam.

"Calm yo' ass down, Carla. I done told yo' ass about letting bitches get you out your character," he spat angrily.

"Naw, I told this bitch I was gonna get in her ass next time I saw her, and before you say it, I know the bitch is pregnant, but her damn face ain't." She was standing over there with her hands on her hips like she had some shit to say.

"Bitch, you got some shit to say? Spit the shit out!" I yelled at her silly looking ass.

"Look, you have Sam now, and I don't want no parts of this. I hope y'all have a happy life, but remember what I told you before. He is gonna get tired of you just like he did me, so don't get comfortable." Her scary ass walked off.

"Oh, bitch, you scared, but that's OK. When you have that baby, that ass is mine!" I yelled. I knew for a fact she was about to go to the police station, but I didn't give a damn because like I had told her, once she had that baby, she would be seeing me.

Walking off, I made my way to Summer's room. Sam was on my heels, and I knew he was about to start some shit. I didn't care what he was talking about, though; I had murder on my mind. I thought Sam had handled that shit, but evidently, he hadn't.

"Listen, baby, you can't keep letting that girl get to you. You know all I want is yo' mean ass." He pulled me into his body, and I melted into his embrace.

"I know, but I told her ratchet ass that every time I saw her, I was gonna tag her ass. She is so damn disrespectful, and you know I don't take disrespect lightly." He was so damn sexy to me, and the way he had his dreads pulled back was even sexier. My pussy started throbbing. All I wanted him to do was bend me over and fuck the shit out of me.

"Get your mind out the gutta. The look on your face tells it all. All yo' ass thinks about is the dick. I could take you in the bathroom and fuck the shit out of you, but right now is not the time. I got you when we get home." He winked at me.

How did this nigga know what I was thinking? I swear he does too much. Getting myself together, we headed back to Summer's room hand in hand. Sam was just what I was looking for. Someone I could be myself around, and he wouldn't judge me. I yearned for somebody like him, and since he was all mine now, I was not letting him go. No matter how mad we were at each other, we promised to just talk it out. There was no breaking up.

Once we entered the room, Troy was in bed, holding Summer while she slept. I wanted what they had. Since Summer was asleep, we decided to head to the house.

Giving Summer a quick kiss on the forehead, we were out the door.

Getting to the house, I had one thing on my mind, and that was dick. After we made it in the house, I closed the door, and I was all over Sam. Pulling his dick out of his pants, I spit on it. Taking it into my mouth, I started licking it like a lollipop. Deciding not to give him too much, I started slow. Speeding up, I started deep throating his dick. Sam was moaning like a little bitch, but I knew I was doing the damn thing. Placing my hand under my dress, I started fingering my clit. Plunging in and out, I felt my nut rise while I sucked the skin off Sam's dick. Once he released, I released right behind him. Sticking my fingers into my mouth, my pussy tasted sweet. As soon as he released, his dick got back hard again, and I knew he was about to put that work in. Picking me up and throwing me in the chair, he walked over and lined his dick up with my pussy. When his dick entered me, I almost came all over his dick. He backed out of me, and I knew why.

"Damn, girl, you 'bout to make a nigga nut just by entering that sweet pussy."

While he was standing there, looking at me, I fingered my clit, and it didn't take me long to release. Sticking my fingers into Sam's mouth, he sucked my juices off my finger. His ass was just as freaky as I was, and I think that was why we clicked. Entering me, he started fucking me slowly, but he knew better than that. I started moving my hips, matching his thrusts. Easing out of me, I climbed on top, and it was all over. I started bouncing my ass up and down on his dick. Twisting my nipples, I rode the wave. I wasn't finished with him, though. Winding my hips, he started fucking me from the bottom. He knew how to make me cum in two seconds. Next thing I knew, I felt my juices running down my leg. Sam flipped me over and started sucking the soul out of me. Closing my eyes, I enjoyed the way his lips felt on my pussy. Cumming hard, he made sure to lick me clean.

"Toot that ass up. Let me get it from the back." He didn't have to tell me twice. I tooted my ass up.

"Damn, that's a beautiful sight."

He plunged into my pussy, and I matched his strokes. I swear if he ever tried to leave me, I would cut his dick off, then he could go. There was no way in hell I was going to let another bitch have something that belonged to me. With a couple of deeper strokes, Sam nut all in me, and I wasn't mad at him. Pulling out of me, Sam went and got a warm washcloth and cleaned me up. I was sore as hell, and I knew I was about to be out for the count. Once Sam cleaned his dick, he scooped me up and took me into the bedroom. He laid me down on the bed, laid beside me, and I melted into Sam's embrace.

"I want you to know that you don't have to worry about me going anywhere. You're it for me," he whispered in my ear, and my heart smiled.

"I know. Same here, baby. Promise me that before you cheat on me, you'll let me go. I have dealt with a lot of shit in my life, and all I want is to be happy. When I'm with you, I'm happy," I cried. Sam was more than he knew to me. I wouldn't call it love just yet, but it was close.

"Look at me, baby. I'ma tell you this one last time; I won't ever hurt you. I want to see you happy, so you don't have to worry about that. I done been with a lot of females, and none of them made me feel the way you make me feel. So, you don't have to ever feel like I'ma leave you because that's not the case. You might as well get used to me because I'm here for the long run." He kissed me on the forehead, and I laid my head on his chest. Next thing I knew, I was out.

Waking up, I heard Sam on the phone. I knew it had to be Troy because he never mentioned anyone else around me. Easing out the bed, I limped into the bathroom to relieve my bladder. I needed to soak Miss Kitty. Wiping, I got up and washed my hands. Turning the water on, once it got to the right temperature, I put the stopper in. Waiting for it to fill up, I went back to my room and got a matching bra and panty set. I wasn't going anywhere until later, so I was just going to lay around the house. I needed to check on Summer and the kids, too. Going back into the bathroom, I stepped into the tub. Once my body got used to the temperature, I laid my head back and relaxed. Not even ten minutes into my relaxation, Sam walked in and kissed me on the forehead.

"Baby, I got some things to handle, but I'll be back later. You need anything while I'm out?" he asked.

Poking my lips out, I pouted like a two-year-old. "No, but can you hurry back? I miss you already."

"Put your lips back in. Daddy will be back." The way he said that woke my pussy up, and I felt a tingle between my legs. Kissing me on the lips, he left out the bathroom.

Washing and rinsing a couple of times, I got out and wrapped the towel around my body. Heading toward the front door, I made sure Sam had locked it. Ever since Trent had come into my house, I had been paranoid. When Sam leaves, I know he locks up, but I must check for myself.

Turning on the TV, I decided to catch up on *When Loving You is Wrong*. I had been so busy, I hadn't been keeping up with it. Pausing the TV, I went into the kitchen and looked in the fridge for something to eat. I was hungry, and I didn't remember the last time I had eaten. Pulling the grapes out, I headed back to the living room. Getting comfortable on the chair, I hit the play button. Randal's ass was crazy as hell. This was the episode where he and the man he had sex with in college got into it. He needed to get his shit together. He knew Alex didn't want him like that anymore since she had her husband back and he needed to accept it. He reminded me so much of Trent and the shit he does.

Getting myself together, I needed to head back over to the hospital. Throwing on some yoga pants and a top, I grabbed my keys and was out the door. When I made it to the car, all four tires were flat, and *bitch* was keyed on the driver's side door. I knew exactly who had done it, and I was about to get off in her ass. Pacing back and forth on the lawn, I dialed Sam first. When he answered, I went off.

"Sam, I know this bitch keyed my car and flattened my tires. When I catch her, I'm getting in her ass. Damn, I can't catch a break. I was on my way to see Summer, and this shit happened." I was pissed. Why was this bitch trying to test me? She just didn't get it. I wish she would hurry up and have the baby though because she was going to get this ass whooping.

"Calm down, baby, I'm on the way. Give me about fifteen minutes, and I'll be there. Go in the house and lock the door. Don't open it up for nobody." The way he said it sent chills down my spine.

"Hurry up, baby, visiting hours will be over soon. I wanna hold the babies," I pouted as I made my way inside the house. When I entered the house, I heard something fall inside my bedroom. I wasn't a scary bitch, but at the moment, I was scared.

"Baby, I'll be pulling up in five minutes." He hung up.

Creeping into the bedroom, I didn't see anyone. Grabbing the bat I kept behind the door, I peeped in my closet, and couldn't believe my eyes. It was my mother, and she looked like she was fiending for drugs. I wanted to feel sorry for her, but my heart couldn't.

"How did you get in here? Or better yet, how did you find out where I lived?" I asked with my hands on my hips.

"Please, baby, I need a couple of dollars to get something to eat." She was shaking, and her skin ashy. I knew better, but I wanted her to get the fuck out of my house before Sam got back.

"All I have is ten dollars; you can take that and get the hell out. Don't come back or I will beat your ass. How dare you come up in here after all the shit you put me through. Fuck you and give me my money back." I snatched the money out of her hands, and when I did, she charged at me.

"Little bitch, you always thought you were better than me, but you ain't shit. I don't regret what I let all those men do to you. Fuck me? No, fuck you, little bitch." She repeatedly slapped me in the face. All the things she said brought back memories. Pushing her off me, I started punching her in the face. All the anger I had for her, I released it by repeatedly hitting her.

Zoning out, I forgot this woman was my mother. I beat her ass like she owed me money and Sam ran in and pulled me off her. Getting myself together, I spit on her ass. She was dead to me, and if after today I didn't see her anymore, that was fine by me. She laid on the floor, all bloody, but I didn't give a damn. That was for all the men she had let take advantage of me.

"What the hell is going on here?" Sam barked at me.

"Nothing, but she needs to get the hell out of my house before I go get my gun and shoot her ass." I was dead ass serious.

"Ma'am, no disrespect, but you need to bounce up out of here." He was being nice, and that rubbed me the wrong way.

"Now get the fuck out of my house!" She got up off the floor and ran out the house. She knew not to play with me.

"Are you gonna tell me what that was about?" Sam stood by the door with his face balled up.

"That was my no-good mother. She let men take advantage of me when I was younger so she could get high. She was never there for me, and this is the first time I have seen her in thirteen years." I felt the tears threatening to fall, but I wouldn't give her the pleasure, though.

"Damn, baby, I'm sorry. Come here." Sam hugged me tightly. At this point, I didn't want to go anywhere. All I wanted to do was lay under Sam.

"You still wanna go to the hospital? I can drive you up there."

"Naw, I'm good. I'll call Summer and let her know I'll be by first thing in the morning. All I want is for you to hold me." I was in my feelings.

"Whatever you want, baby, you know I got you." Sam stripped out of his clothes, laid in the bed and patted my side. I got in and moved closer to him. Sam calmed me, and I liked that. Within a few minutes, I drifted off to sleep.

Chapter 11

Sam

I was just getting into a deep sleep when my phone started ringing off the hook. I was just going to let it ring, but my mind told me I needed to answer it. Looking down at the caller ID, I saw it was Craig calling. Whatever he wanted, it had better be important. It was damn near six in the morning. Looking to my left, Carla was sleeping so peacefully. Easing out the bed, I left out the room and took the call.

"Talk to me."

"Damn, nigga, it took your ass long enough to answer the phone." He laughed into the phone.

"Man, I'm tired as hell, so this better be important." All this laughing and shit, he needed to say what the fuck he had to say.

"Nigga, I got a plan to get Shaq's ass. Meet me at Waffle House on the Westside," he told me just before he hung up.

I had forgotten all about that nigga; it was like his ass had disappeared. He wasn't making any noise because he knew that once Troy found his ass, it was all over. Hell, I would hide, too. Troy was crazy about Summer, and he knew that, so I didn't know what had made him try to kill them. I could only imagine what Troy had planned for him. Getting back to the room, I saw that Carla wasn't in there, so that meant she was in the tub, soaking. I had put a hurting on that pussy. Opening the bathroom door, she was laying in the tub with her eyes closed. Damn, she was so sexy. Moving close to her, I bent down and kissed her on the forehead and told her I would be back later. She tried to act up, but she knew better than that. Making my way out the house, I got in the car. Driving over to Waffle House, I plotted out my next steps with Carla. I couldn't see myself with anyone else, so maybe it was time for me to settle down and have a couple of kids. I wanted her to be my wife. I wanted us to be more than boyfriend and girlfriend. Carla was a nigga's heart.

Making it to Waffle House, I parked and got out the car. Craig was already inside eating. Shaking my head, I headed inside. Getting to the table, he wiped his hands off and dapped me up.

"Damn, nigga, you couldn't wait for me before you started eating," I joked with him.

"You know me, nigga; I have to eat." He shook his head.

After I ordered something to eat, we started talking. I knew this nigga couldn't be this hungry. He had ordered himself something else. I didn't know where it was going because he was skinny as fuck. I didn't want to say too much until my food came and I took a couple of bites. I didn't realize I was that hungry until my food made it to the table.

"So, I know that y'all know I'm messing with Shaq's baby mama so I can bring his ass to y'all." I was now all ears.

"Word, I forgot about that shit. Bring his ass to us then." He was talking, but I wanted him to show us.

"I am, but I gotta get in good with her again, though. I kinda pissed her off, and she told me she wasn't fucking with me no more." He shook his head. This nigga here. I swear he was a damn fool.

"What the fuck you mean, she ain't fucking with you no more? How the hell you supposed to get us Shaq is all I

He was starting to piss me off. He got me
lling me he could get us Shaq, now he was
different.

panties out a bunch, I got a plan. Don't
worry, we will be good in a couple of days. They don't stay
where they used to no more, but her number still the same.
I won't let you niggas down, you know we go back."

"Nigga, get us Shaq's ass, or that's your ass. Don't play,
nigga." At this point, I was mad as hell. This nigga wasn't
talking about anything. Hell, I could have kept my ass in
bed with Carla.

Carla had called me and told me someone had keyed her
ride and I hoped Rhonda didn't have shit to do with this. I
tried to give her a warning, but she didn't want to take my
hint. Carla had already told her once she had her baby, it
was going to be on and popping.

Making it to the house, I got out the car and locked up.
Getting to the door, I inserted the key and entered, and
something felt off. I couldn't quite put my finger on it.
Slowly approaching the bedroom, I heard Carla talking shit
to somebody. Finally getting to the room, Carla was tearing
off into what looked like her mama's ass. I mean, they
looked just alike. Pulling her off the woman, she told her
to get out. I had never seen her this mad, and I didn't know
what the fuck was going on. Pulling her into me, she cried
on my chest, and that shit tugged a nigga's heart. When she
got herself together, she told me about her life and how her
mother had done her and I wanted to run after her and bust
a cap in her ass. Now it all made sense. Carla was a broken
woman who had been through shit in life that no one
should go through. She had been abused and raped her
whole life. *Damn, ain't that some shit.*

"Baby, calm down. I got you no matter what. I don't care about your past, let's focus on the future." I was dead ass serious. I didn't care about her past. I could picture us growing old together.

"You still wanna be with me after what I just told you?" She sniffled and looked at me with sad eyes.

"Hell yes! That don't stop the way I'm feeling your ass. Didn't I tell you when we first started talking that you were gonna be my wife?" She was all a nigga wanted, broken and all, and I was going to do everything in my power to make her happy.

I didn't want my baby to go through the shit she had been through anymore, and I was going to protect her from any and everything. I wanted her to be comfortable enough to come and talk to me. Right now, she was shutting me out, but that wasn't going to last forever. It was a little after 7:30 P.M., and we didn't have shit to do so we were going to lay up and watch movies all day. I had already told Troy I wasn't going to be able to come in today, but he had just hired an older lady named Minnie, and she was cool as shit. She didn't mind opening and closing the shop.

Snapping out of my thoughts, my baby walked out the bathroom looking sexy as fuck. Her hair was all over the place, but she still made my dick hard. I could look at other women, but they couldn't do the shit Carla did to me. She walked up and stood between my legs, and I could tell something was on her mind.

"Talk to me, baby. What's on your mind?" She looked at me and kissed my lips. I knew she didn't want to talk about it, and I wasn't going to force her. I knew once she felt the time was right, she would come and talk to me.

"Nothing, baby. I'm good. How was your day, though?" I

could see right through Carla; she always switched it to me.

"It was good, baby. I'm better now that I'm with you. I thought we could go house hunting. Like, me and you staying together. I know we do that now, but I want a house that we can grow old in." That smile on her face told it all; she didn't have to say it.

"You know I'm good with that. I was wondering when we were gonna get to that level. I see how you bring yourself over here, piece by piece." I laughed. She had caught a nigga.

"I'll get with the realtor that Troy and Summer used. Maybe we can find something close to them. I know Summer would love for y'all to be next door neighbors." She was going to need help with the twins when Troy was at work so that would be perfect since she doesn't have any other family or friends that she talks about.

"That would be great. Let me call Summer and tell her we are about to be neighbors," she squealed. She kissed me on the lips and ran off. While she was on the phone, I decided to get up and take a shower. Going over to the dresser where I kept my stuff, I got out a pair of boxers and tank top. Once I had everything I needed, I went into the bathroom, looked around and smiled. I had a toothbrush and other shit over here. It was like we lived together, but I wanted something with both of our names on it. Turning the water on, I waited for it to heat up before I got in. While I was waiting for it to get hot, I brushed my teeth. When I got in the shower, the water was hot as shit, and it burned a nigga. I jumped back quickly, adjusting the water, and now it was perfect. I washed every inch of my body a couple of times, then got out. I was ready to lay under my baby. After drying off, I slipped on my boxers and tank top. Getting my clothes, I threw them into the dirty clothes basket. When I made it back in the room, Carla was laid in the bed, comfortable and shit. She was snuggled up like she was cold. She pulled the cover back and patted my side, and I wasted no time diving in the bed.

"What you in here watching, baby? You know we not 'bout to watch that girly shit tonight. We gonna watch a nigga movie tonight." I playfully snatched the remote from her.

"I don't wanna watch that. Let's just watch this." She tried to pout, but I gave her a look, and she changed that quickly.

"Carla, I told you about that pouting shit. Your ass ain't three no more. You too grown to be pouting, ma." I threw the remote back at her. She better be glad I love her ass.

Chapter 12

Troy

A nigga was happy. Baby girl was finally ready to come home. Summer and Jr. had been released from the hospital, but Tay wasn't big enough. That was a tough pill to swallow, leaving the hospital and leaving her there. It was like we were still there because we visited her every day. Jr. was giving us hell because I think he had gotten used to his sister, and without her, he wasn't himself. I was glad to have both of them home together. The crazy thing is, Jr. looked just like Summer, and Tay looked just like me. Weird, but I loved them.

I needed to get to the shop and check on things, but I wasn't going to leave them there alone. Picking up my phone, I dialed Sam to see if Carla could come over until I got back. I wasn't going to be gone long, I just wanted to make sure the shop was running smoothly. When Sam told me Carla would be over in a little while, I got up to take a shower. Summer was in the room with the kids, making sure they were good. Peeking my head through the door, she was breastfeeding Jr. His little ass knew he could eat. He was already a titty baby. When the nipple wasn't in his mouth, he cried.

Walking over to the crib, I picked up Tay. She was light as her and at first, I thought I was going to drop her with how small she was. Summer had to show me how to hold her. Once I got that down packed, I was okay. Baby girl sucked her thumb, and I didn't like it, but I knew she was going to do it.

"Little mama, you hungry?" I cooed at my daughter. She had the chubbiest cheeks. When she smiled at me, that melted my heart.

"Baby, I think Tay is hungry. How 'bout we switch. You give me Jr. and take Tay." Jr. was spoiled as shit. He didn't want anyone to hold him but Summer. When we first got home, Summer was cleaning up, and I had to pick him up because he was crying. He cried like someone was killing him, but as soon as Summer came and got him, he stopped crying. I could already tell he was going to be a mama's boy.

Once we switched, I sat down on the couch that we had in their room and played with Jr. He was calm for the time being, but I knew that wasn't going to last long. As I thought, Jr. started screaming his head off. I got my ass up and gave him back to Summer. I knew I was going to have to start helping Summer more with him, but all that screaming, I couldn't do. I could keep baby girl all day because she was chill. She only cried when she was hungry or wet, but other than that, she was a great baby.

Walking over to Summer, I gave her Jr. and took Tay from her. Kissing her on the forehead, I walked back over to the couch and sat down with Tay. It all felt unreal. I was somebody's daddy. I wouldn't change this feeling for anything in the world. Playing with Tay for a little while longer, I placed her back in her crib. I needed to get ready to head out.

"Baby, I gotta go out for a little bit. Carla is gonna come over for a little while till I get back." She was relieved when I said that. I knew she wasn't ready to stay with the twins alone, and with everything going on, I wouldn't leave them alone.

"OK, baby! The twins and I will be here when you get back. I love you!" She blew me an air kiss.

"I love you, too, baby. Let me hop in the shower, Carla should be here in a minute."

Leaving out of the room, I headed to our bedroom. Once inside, I went to my dresser and got out some underclothes. Going into the bathroom, I turned the water on and waited for it to get to temperature. I brushed and flossed while it got hot. Stepping into the shower, the water relaxed me, and I started thinking about what I wanted to do to Summer in here. I was so backed up, so once those six weeks were up, she would most likely get pregnant again. I couldn't wait to be balls deep in her pussy. My dick stood at attention.

"Down boy, it ain't even that kind of that party," I told my dick. I only craved Summer.

Washing a couple of times, I got out the shower. Wrapping a towel around me, I walked into the bedroom and Summer was sitting on the side of the bed, deep in thought.

"Baby, what's wrong?" I asked, walking up to her.

"Nothing, just got a lot on my mind." I stood there, all ears.

"Talk to me, baby."

"What if he comes back for me?" The way she had fear in her voice pissed me off. This nigga had to be dealt with. I had forgotten all about his bitch ass.

"Don't worry about that, baby. I got you." I cupped the bottom of her chin and kissed her. That kiss sent a message to my dick, but I knew now wasn't the right time.

Pulling away from the kiss, I had business to tend to. Shaq was about to get what was coming to him. As soon as I found his ass, I was putting a bullet through his skull. We had people looking for his ass, but his ass had gotten ghost.

He couldn't hide forever. He was going to slip, and I couldn't wait for that day. I was ready to have a normal life. Summer and the kids deserved that, and I was going to do everything in my power to give them the world. I was about to stop playing and make Summer my wife. As soon as I got done handling business, I was going ring shopping. I needed to get with Carla though so she could help a nigga out. Throwing on something comfortable, I waited for Carla to get here. I wasn't working today, I just needed to check on things. Hearing the doorbell ring, I jumped up and headed downstairs. Opening the door, Carla was standing on the other side.

"What's good, sis?" I pulled her in for a hug.

"Nothing much, bruh, just life." I could tell she had been crying because her eyes were red and sad.

"I'm sorry, sis. I hope my nigga ain't messing up. You know I can get him straight for you." I was dead ass serious. Sam would be a fool to mess up what he and Carla had.

"Naw, nothing like that. My mother came by today, and all the anger I had built up for her, I released it. Sam didn't know about my past, and once I told him, he still wanted me. I've been through a lot of shit in life, but none of that matters to Sam. It's just too good to be true. I wanna give my all to him, but I'm scared as hell." I could see the fear in her eyes.

"Sis, I'ma tell you like this, Sam is not that kinda nigga. If he's with you, he's with you. He done been through some deep shit, too. I think that's why y'all click like that. I'm telling you, me and Sam have been friends for a minute, and when he loves, he loves hard. Open up to him so y'all can grow together." I was being honest with her. I had never seen Sam this happy. I know for sure he loves her ass because that was all he talked about.

"I know, bruh. Thanks for the talk. Things are gonna get better. I'm not going anywhere, and he ain't, either. He made that known earlier," she laughed.

"Check this out, though, sis. I need your help. I think it's time for me and Summer to take the next step and I need your help picking out the perfect ring for her."

Covering her mouth so she wouldn't squeal, she said, "Of course. I would be honored to help you out. I'm so happy for you guys." She walked over to me and gave me a sisterly hug. "Welcome to the family brother-in-law." She ran off to go upstairs where Summer was.

"Carla!" I called out after her, stopping her dead in her tracks. "Keep this between you and me. I want to surprise her."

"You got it. Your secret is safe with me." She zipped her mouth, threw the key away, and proceeded upstairs. Sis was wild. I made a mental note to call Sam and see what was up with him. I liked Carla for him; she calmed his ass down. I also needed to get Summer's push present in order, but Craig was handling that for me. I made sure to tell him she didn't want a minivan, but he would get one just to be petty. Shaking my head, I left out the house.

Locking the door, I made my way to the car, and I was off to the shop. When I got there, it was jamming as always. Parking my car, I got out and headed into the store. Going into the shop, Lacy was sitting at the desk, looking ratchet and shit, and she was giving her gum hell.

"What's good, Lacy? How has business been around here?" She stopped smacking and looked up at me, and I could see the lust in her eyes, but this dick belonged to Summer.

"It's been good, boss man. Congratulations on the babies."

"Appreciate it. Let me get back here and do a little work so I can get back home." I caught her looking at my dick print. She wasn't even trying to hide that shit. Shaking my head, I left and went to my office.

Once I got in the office, I turned on the computer and got to work. Not even fifteen minutes later, Lacy walked into my office. This bitch had some nerve; she didn't even knock. Closing the door, she locked it. Lacy wasn't ugly, she was just ratchet as hell with purple hair. Making her way to my desk, she moved my laptop out the way and sat in front of me. She spread her legs, and I saw that she didn't have any drawers on. Her pussy was pretty and smelled good, but I wasn't about to fuck up what Summer and I had.

"Bossman, I know you aren't getting any pussy at home, and I'm here to take care of you." She pushed my chair back and dropped to her knees, and I sat back and watched the show. I knew I was wrong, but I was a nigga at the end of the day.

She was sucking the skin off my dick. Bobbing her head, I grabbed a fistful of hair. I felt my nut rise, so I started fucking her face. Releasing my nut, I got up and went into the bathroom to clean my dick. Cleaning my dick off, I felt disgusted, but I couldn't help myself. I needed a quick release, but this shit couldn't happen anymore. I knew for a fact it wasn't because I was about to fire Lacy's ass, even if I had to come in and work up front until I found her replacement. I was about to start hiring old women because this couldn't keep happening. Walking out the bathroom, Lacy's ass was on top of my desk, fingering her clit. She had a pretty pussy, but I couldn't go there with her. It was bad enough she knew what my dick looked and tasted like.

"Lacy, you are gonna have to get out my office with that, and while you at it, you need to be looking for another job. I will give you a month to find a job, and while you are looking, I will pay you. After the thirty days, the checks stop." She was still finger fucking herself. She sped up, and I knew she was getting closer to her nut. Seeing her juices flow out of her pussy had me wanting to bend her ass over this desk.

"Lacy, you need to get the fuck off my desk and out my damn office. Who the fuck is at the desk while your ass is back here, trying to give your pussy away? Get the fuck back up there, and you need to be looking on the internet for another job." I shook my head at her ass.

"Troy, so you're firing me? I was just trying to help you out since I know you ain't getting any pussy at home," she smirked.

"It ain't none of your damn business if I ain't getting no pussy at home. You are wrong on all levels. Get the fuck out before I cut you off altogether." She had managed to piss me off with that mouth of hers.

"I wonder what Summer would say if she found out you out here slanging dick," she smirked, and I wanted to choke her ass. I swear bitches were always trying to do spiteful shit.

"Summer won't know anything about this, and if she finds out, then that's yo' ass." If looks could kill, she would be one dead bitch. That was what was wrong with bitches these days: they couldn't keep their mouths close. I knew I was wrong, but damn.

When she left the room, she made it known she had an

attitude because she slammed my damn door. Grabbing my phone out of my pocket, I saw that I had dialed Summer by mistake. Damn, I was in some deep shit. I hoped like hell she hadn't heard any of that shit. Redialing her number, she answered on the second ring, sounding happy, so I knew she hadn't heard anything.

"Hey, baby!" she cooed.

"Hey, baby, how are the kids?" I asked, being a concerned daddy.

"They are good, baby, but what time are you coming home? I miss you."

"Let me finish up here, and then I'm on my way, baby."

"OK, bae. I love you, and hurry up."

"Love you, too!" I told her just before I hung up.

Rushing to get done with what I was doing, I needed to get home to my family. I needed to call Sam and see if he minded sitting with Summer and the kids while Carla helped me pick out a ring. I knew he wouldn't mind, but I wanted to ask anyway. I also wanted to know what was going on with him and Sis.

Hearing my phone ring, I looked down, and it was Erica. I hadn't heard from her in a minute, so maybe it was about the appointment to get the DNA test. Wasting no time, I answered.

"What's good, E! Everything OK with the baby?" I asked, concerned.

"My water just broke, and I don't have anyone to take me to the hospital. The contractions are very strong, so please hurry. I don't wanna have her here." She sounded like she was crying.

"I'm on my way. Give me about fifteen minutes," I told her and hung up.

I sent Summer a text, letting her know that Erica was in labor and I needed to get her to the hospital. She replied with OK. She was taking the situation better as the days went by. She knew I didn't want Erica's ass like that. If this was my child, I would be there for her, but as far as Erica went, I didn't want her like that. Closing all the apps on the computer, I was out the door. Lacy shot daggers at my ass, but I didn't give a fuck.

"Lock up. I gotta handle some business. Remember what I told you, too."

Before she could open her mouth, I was out the door. Getting in my car, I rushed to get to Erica's apartment. Hell, I didn't know why she had gone out and gotten an apartment when I told her ass she could have the house. Hell, it was paid for, but she wasn't hearing that shit.

Getting to her place, I jumped out the car and headed inside. Knocking on the door, I heard her say it was open. Entering the house, Erica was laid on the floor on her back.

"Come on, E, we need to get you to the hospital." She had on little-ass shorts and her bra, so I knew I had to get her dressed. Looking at her had my dick harder than a motherfucker. It was crazy that she still had that effect on me.

"Troy, can you go get me something to throw on and stop eye-fucking me!" she yelled.

"Girl, chill out with that shit. Ain't nobody eye-fucking you. Tell me where your room is so I can get you something to put on." She had caught me, but hell, you couldn't blame me. Erica was fine as hell, but I couldn't take it there with her.

"Second door to the left. Please hurry up," she said between grunts.

Rushing to the room, I picked something for her to wear. Making it back to the living room, I helped her get dressed. Within ten minutes, we were out the door, and it took us no time to get to the hospital. They wheeled her back and told us she was fully dilated. She pushed three times and out came a beautiful baby girl. She weighed six pounds and three ounces and was twenty inches long. Taking a look at her, I knew she wasn't mine. She looked like she had Down Syndrome, but that didn't matter. When I held baby girl, I didn't feel what I felt when I held my daughter. They swabbed me for the DNA test and told me they were going to put a rush on it. I didn't even say bye to Erica, I just left. I was going to wait until the test came back before I started bonding with her, though.

Getting in the car, I headed over to Kay's. Before I got there, I called Sam to see if he could stay with Summer and the kids till I got back. Dialing Carla, I asked her to meet me at the mall once Sam got there. It didn't matter the price; Summer deserved it all. It wasn't like I was hurting for money, anyway.

Arriving at Kay's, I waited in the car for Carla. In my mind, I replayed what had gone down with Lacy, and the guilt started to sink in. I was going to take that to the grave with me, and I hoped like hell none of it was on Summer's voicemail. When Carla got there, we headed inside the store and started looking around.

"You know the ring size doesn't matter to Summer, as long

as she has you," Carla emphasized. To me, it mattered. I wanted my baby to have it all.

"I know, sis, I just want her to be happy. Diamonds are a girl's best friend, right?" I smirked, and she just laughed.

"You right, but I'm telling you, Summer is not that kind of girl. You can get her a simple rock, and she would be happy."

I heard everything she said, but I wanted what I wanted. If I had to spend a grip on the perfect ring for her, I would. I had enough money to buy her the world if she wanted it. I spotted the perfect ring, and it was a 1 3/8 carat Neil Lane Diamond Engagement ring. It cost almost $5,000, and I knew she would like it. Looking over at Carla, she nodded her head and was cheesing harder than a motherfucker. Having the salesman wrap it up for me, I made my way to the register to pay for it. Once I paid for it, I slipped it into my pocket and headed for the door.

"I'm thinking about having a dinner Sunday to propose to her. Will you and Sam be able to make it?"

"I'm there. You know I wouldn't miss this for anything in the world. You about to make my sister the happiest woman in the world," she grinned.

"That's the plan. I don't see me being with anyone else. Summer makes me happy, and she gave me my kids, so I'm about to make her a Davis," I grinned. A nigga was happy. I had everything a man could ask for.

"Don't hurt my sister. If you do, you're gonna have to deal with me." Carla held up her little ass fist. She had nothing to worry about, though. Summer was in good hands. Speaking of Summer, my phone went off, and it was her.

"Baby, I'm on the way home, is there anything you need before I get there?" I asked all in one sentence.

"No, I'm good, just wanted to know what time you would be here. We need to talk." When she said those words, my palms started sweating. I knew it was about the shit that had happened earlier. I was scared to lose her and the kids.

"I'm on my way. I should be there in fifteen minutes. I love you."

"OK," was all she said before she hung up. *Fuck man, how could this be happening?*

Thanking Carla, we went our separate ways. My mind was all over the place. I wanted to go ahead and tell her, but at the same time, I didn't. A nigga's heart was beating out of my chest, and I wasn't ready for whatever Summer wanted to talk about.

On the ride to the house, I dialed Craig to see if he had anything for me yet. He picked up on the first ring. Damn, this nigga must have thought I was someone else.

"Damn, man, let the phone ring a little bit. No, on the real, though, I was calling to see if you found me a truck yet. I kind of need it ASAP. No rush, though." I heard him laugh.

"Yeah, about that, I found a 2017 Dodge Durango with black insides. Summer would love it. Hell, when I sat in it, I fell in love. You can look at it if you want to. It's at the Dodge dealership on Lancaster." This was why I fucked with him. He was always on it.

"Cool, let me go home and see what Summer wants. I'll get up with you later, though." I ended the call and proceeded to the house.

Chapter 13

Summer

This nigga had some nerve to tell me he loved me and then let another bitch suck his dick. Yeah, I opened the voicemail as soon as Carla left. Bitches weren't shit these days. I didn't know why I thought Troy was going to be any different than Shaq, but that was my fault, though. I just couldn't find the right man to save my life. I found it strange that when Sam came over, Carla left, and they didn't exchange words or anything. That alone told me there was trouble in paradise.

Making sure the kids were situated, I made my way into the living room to chat with Sam. Walking in there, he looked like he had lost his best friend. Sam was a handsome man, he just wasn't my type. His ass was a little too bright for me. I mean, don't get me wrong, Shaq was bright, but that was different.

"Sam, what's wrong, bruh? You know you can talk to me about anything," I told him, taking a seat on the couch beside him. I put a pillow between us to give us space.

"Man, sis, I don't know what's going on. Like, one minute, Carla is all in with me, and the next, she is pulling away. She told me about her past, and I still love her. Matter of fact, I love her a little more for opening up to me. The way she is pushing me away, I don't think we are gonna make it. Man, I love the hell out of your sister." Sam sounded hurt.

"Yep, that's Carla. She is stubborn, and I can tell you that once things start to seem like it's more than a friend, she falls back. That's how she's been for as long as I have known her. What did she tell you about her past?"

"Today, she called me and told me someone had keyed her car, and I went over. I walked into the house, and something was off, but I couldn't put my finger on it, though. So, I made it to her room, and she was beating the hell out of a lady. From the looks of it, she could be her mother. Anyway, I pulled her off her, and she told her to leave. After she was gone, she told me that her mother would let men take advantage of her when she was younger. Carla broke down on a nigga, and when I tell you I wanted to find her and bust a cap in her ass, that's exactly what I wanted to do. Once she was all cried out, I told her I wasn't going anywhere so she might as well get used to seeing me. I thought we were all good, but she keeps shutting me out. I don't know what to do anymore." I saw the hurt in Sam's eyes.

"Damn, I didn't know she was going through all that. She told me about some of her past, but not all of it. All I can say is give her time, and she will come around." Now I was hurt because I was supposed to be her bestie slash sister, someone she was supposed to come to when she needed a shoulder to lean on, and she hadn't confided in me.

"I am. She can try to push me away all she wants, but I'm here to stay. Enough about me, what's going on with you, sis?"

"I'm here at the house, and Troy told me he was going to handle business. That was OK with me because when I met him, he told me he was a business. Anyway, getting to the juicy part, he called me by mistake, and he was getting his dick sucked by another bitch. She threatened to tell me once she got fired, and Troy told her he would kill her if she did. I love Troy, don't get me wrong, but I will not take the shit I went through with Shaq." He had asked, and I wasn't sugarcoating anything. That was something about Sam; I could talk to him without judgment.

"I told Troy that Lacy was gonna be a problem when we first opened the shop. I saw the way she would look at him, and he would never give her the time of day. I'm not trying to take up for him, don't get me wrong, but sometimes, we think with the wrong head. I can tell you this, though; Troy loves the hell out of you. When he talks about you, I can see that sparkle in his eyes. Don't give up on him, because at the end of the day, these bitches out here don't wanna see nobody happy. They are forever trying to break up a happy home. Let him explain, and y'all go from there. Please, Summer, don't take the kids from him. That nigga would lose his mind." I believed everything Sam had said.

"Don't worry, I won't take the kids from him. I will give him a chance to explain, and we will go from there. I just don't want to be the person to get hurt in the long run." This talk with Sam was just what I needed. He was so sincere and honest with me.

Just as I was about to go into the kitchen to make the twins a bottle, Tay screamed at the top of her lungs. I knew it was her because she had a high pitch scream. Jr.'s scream was normal. Rushing upstairs to their room, Tay was soaking wet, and Jr. was lying beside her, blowing bubbles. I picked up Tay and took her to the bathroom. Placing her in the baby tub, I cleaned her up. Now she was as happy as she could be. Getting her an outfit out the closet, I lotioned her little body, and she was settled and calm now. Sam had gotten Jr. out the crib, and I needed to strip the sheets and wash them. Pulling the sheets off the bed, I threw them on the floor. Sam was sitting in the corner with Jr.; he was so good with him. I knew once Carla stopped playing and blessed him with one, he was going to be an amazing father.

"I need to run downstairs and get them a bottle. Do you mind watching the kids until I come back?"

"They good, sis. Tell Mama, Uncle got me," he cooed to Jr., and he was eating the attention up.

Troy needed to get his ass here and help me with his kids. He must have heard me talking about his ass because he walked through the door. He looked so sexy with his sweats and Js on, but now wasn't the time to be thinking about his ass like that. I was about to get in his ass once I make sure the kids were straight. He spoke to me and headed upstairs, and I rolled my eyes and got two of the bottles I had made earlier. Sam came downstairs and hugged me.

"Sis, just hear him out. You know he wouldn't hurt you." He pulled away from the hug.

"I ain't gonna make no promises, so he better come correct." I was dead serious. I wasn't about to let his ass off easy. He deserved this cursing out I was about to give him. Giving my dick away, where they do that at?

"All right, sis, take it easy. I'm out." Following him, I locked the door.

When I made it upstairs, Troy was playing with the kids, and it was so cute. Tay was going to be a daddy's girl, and Jr. was going to be a mama's boy. Sam had put new sheets on the bed, so I needed to call him and thank him. Picking up Jr. from the crib, I fed him and burped him. Once I got him squared away, I took Tay from Troy and fed her. I wasn't ready for the argument that was about to go down.

After the kids were all squared away, I got up and went to take a bath. My emotions were all over the place. I wanted to spend the rest of my life with Troy, but at the same time, I didn't want him to treat me like shit. Running the water in the tub, I poured a little vanilla bubble bath in. Waiting for the tub to fill up, I went and got something to slip on. My six weeks were almost up, and I was horny as shit. Troy didn't deserve my goodies, though. Stepping into the tub, I let my head fall back. Lord, I missed my mama so much. She would know what to do about this situation. I wished I could call her and ask her for advice. I couldn't do that though because she was gone, but she was with me spiritually, though. I didn't realize I was crying until a tear hit my ear. Getting myself together, I washed and rinsed my body a couple of times, then I got out and let the water out. Drying off, I exited the bathroom.

Inside the room, Troy was laying down on his side of the bed. Why was this man so damn fine? I didn't want to think about the voicemail, but it replayed over and over in my head. I was tired of getting hurt; I wanted more. Lotioning my body, I grabbed a pair of socks to put on. He could play sleep all he wanted, but I was about to get off in his ass.

"Troy, I know your ass ain't sleep, so get the fuck up. We need to talk." He rolled over and was now facing me.

"Summer, before you start, let me explain. First off, I would like to say I'm sorry that it even happened. Shit, it just happened. It was just head; it didn't mean shit to me. I love you and only you, but I had a weak moment. Please, baby, don't leave me." He was down on his knees, begging.

"I don't know, Troy. Right now, I just need time to think. You hurt me. You gave another bitch something that belongs to me. How would you feel if I gave my pussy to another man? Huh! Answer me, dammit." I was hitting him in his chest, and he just stood there, staring at me.

"I would body that nigga. Don't ever talk about another nigga in front of me." I saw the fire in his eyes, and I think mine matched his. I'd heard what he had said, but talk wasn't worth shit. I wanted him to hurt like I was hurting. I understood it was just head, but that was still sex in my book.

"I don't know, Troy, I need time to think about this. You can sleep in the guest room while I think." I threw his pillow at him.

"OK, you can get that. Take your time. I'm sorry, baby." He walked over and tried to kiss me, and I turned my head, so he kissed my cheek.

Once he was gone, I grabbed my phone and dialed Sarah. I needed her advice about this situation.

"Hello?" she answered, sounding like she was sleeping.

"I'm sorry if I woke you, Ma, but I need you right now."

"Don't worry, baby, it's OK. Talk to me. What is on your mind? Nothing is more important than you." She sounded sincere.

"Ma, I love Troy with all my heart, but he hurt me in a way that I don't think I can forgive him for," I said between tears.

"Summer, whatever he did, I'm sure you guys can fix it. Don't give up on y'all, because, at the end of the day, people want to see you guys fail. Tell me what he did, though." All she was saying was true.

"Today, he told me he was going to work, and he made a mistake of calling me while another woman was sucking his dick. I know it ain't that bad, but it is. I was at home taking care of his kids while he was out his getting his dick sucked. I'm sorry, mama, excuse my language." I stressed to my mom.

"Summer, listen to me and listen to me good. You have an

amazing man, don't let this one mess up mess up y'all's relationship. I'm not saying it's OK for him to do that because it's not. Troy loves you and your dirty draws. Y'all have two beautiful kids to raise, so don't let this break y'all. Give it some time, and this shall pass." If I couldn't depend on anyone to keep it real with me, I could rely on her.

"Thanks, Ma, I appreciate your chat. I'm gonna take your advice, and we will get over this. The kids and I will be by tomorrow to see you. I love you." Honestly, I knew I wasn't going anywhere. Troy was it for me.

"I love you, too, baby, and I can't wait to see y'all tomorrow," she squealed just before she hung up. She was a mess, but that was my mama.

I needed to hear that from her. It felt like a weight had been lifted off my shoulder. I would talk to Troy tomorrow, but right now, I was going to try and get some sleep before the twins woke up. Dozing off, I felt someone get in the bed behind me. I wasn't up for arguing, so I let him hold me. The tighter he held me, the harder I cried.

"Ssshhh, baby, I'm sorry. I never meant to hurt you. Stop crying." He tried to calm me down, but I cried harder.

"You told me you weren't gonna hurt me, but you still managed to do that. What else are you hiding from me?" I sniffled and got myself together.

"Erica had the baby today, but the little girl looks nothing like me. She has Down Syndrome, but she is beautiful, no doubt. I just didn't feel that attachment to her like I did when you had Taylor. We did a DNA test, and hopefully, once it comes back, we can move on with our lives." I was glad that Erica had had the baby, and there was a possibility she wasn't Troy's. It was sad to hear that she had Down Syndrome, though, and I was going to make it my business to check on her tomorrow.

"Well, that's good to know. I want to go to the hospital tomorrow and see if they need anything. I don't mind helping Erica out until we figure this thing out." Honestly, I didn't have a problem with her as long as she stayed in her lane.

"That would be nice. You can be sweet when you want to." Troy kissed me, and the juices between my legs started flowing. I was due to go to the doctor next week for my six-week checkup, but I couldn't wait, my pussy was on fire.

Troy laid me on my back, ripped my thong and started eating my pussy. Damn, I had missed this. His tongue game was on point. His tongue flicked over my pussy and Lord, I felt like I was going to die. I mean, it felt so good, I was squirming all over the bed. He held my body still and went ham. Next thing I knew, I was cumming all over his face, and he licked me clean.

"God damn, girl, this pussy is still sweet like I remembered." He moved closer to me, wiping his mouth off with the back of his hand.

"Troy, I so needed that. Thank you." I rolled over on my side like I was about to go to sleep.

"Oh, naw, baby girl, not yet. I'm about to fuck the shit out of you, then you can go to sleep." He pulled me to the foot of the bed.

When he pulled his dick out, I almost died. His dick was so big and pretty, my damn mouth started watering, but he didn't deserve my head game. Lining his dick up to the opening of my pussy, he pushed his way in. I flinched at first; that shit hurt like hell. The way he was thrusting in and out of me, it felt like he was fucking some shit up. Once he got all the way in, it felt good as shit. The deeper the strokes got, the louder I moaned. Damn, what was this man doing to me? All that could be heard throughout the room was our bodies slapping together. Closing my eyes, I arched my back and rode the wave. Not too long after I came, he came inside me, and I panicked. What would they think of me if I came in for my six-week checkup pregnant? Oh well, shit happens.

"Troy, you know I'm probably pregnant after all that you just dropped in me," I laughed. It was a pretty big load, but he acted like he didn't have a care in the world.

Laughing, he climbed off me and went to the bathroom to get a rag to clean me up. Just that quickly, I had my man back. He wasn't off the hook yet, but this was a start. Once he cleaned me up and changed the sheets, I went to the kids' room to change them. While I was at it, I went ahead and fed them, too. Once I was done, I went back in the room and cuddled with my man.

Chapter 14

Erica

I was sitting here staring at my baby; she was so beautiful to me. I had denied all my visitors because I just wasn't in the mood to talk to anybody. Shaq's stupid ass still hadn't come by to see our daughter. At first, I was going to fill Troy's head up and let him think Shayla was his, but Troy wasn't as stupid as I made him out to be. When he held her, I saw no emotions. No tears of joy or anything. Then he had the nerve to tell me he didn't feel the attachment like he did when Summer had the twins, but I didn't give a damn about that.

Picking up the hospital phone, I redialed Shaq, and it went straight to voicemail like it had been doing since I had called him the first time. Word on the street was he was in hiding, but I didn't give a damn because our daughter needed him. I decided to leave him another voicemail, cursing his ass out. I wasn't going to beg him to be my baby's father. She had me, so that was all that mattered. Shayla started crying, so I got up from the bed and went over to pick her up.

"What's wrong with mama's baby? Are you hungry?" I cooed, and she started popping her lips.

Sitting in the rocker that was brought into my room, I pulled my nipple out and started feeding her. It took no time for her to latch on. She was so greedy. I needed to get a breast pump so I could pump my milk and store it for emergencies. After she had gotten enough, she released my nipple. Sitting her up, I burped her, and she looked sleepy. Getting the blanket from the bassinet, I placed it on her back and started rocking her. I remembered when I was little, and my mother used to sing to me, and I would instantly fall asleep. Just as I was about to sing, I heard a knock at the door. I thought I had told the nurses I didn't want any visitors. People just didn't listen. Maybe if I didn't answer, they would go away. Wishful thinking, the knocking continued. Letting out a sigh, I told whoever was on the other side of the door to come in. I couldn't believe my eyes when Summer and Troy walked in. They were the last people I wanted to see. Stepping in, they placed the gift bag and flowers on the table.

"Damn, Erica, you don't have to be so damn rude, you can speak," Summer spoke. The room was so quiet, you could hear a pin drop.

"Hey, what brings you guys by?" I held Shayla tighter. I didn't want her to see my baby.

"We came to check on you and the baby. How are you guys doing?" She tried to get a peek at Shayla, but I wasn't having that.

"We are doing just fine. Thank y'all for coming by, but y'all can leave now. Shayla is trying to sleep." I didn't mean to be rude, but it is what it is. I wasn't in the mood for them.

"Damn, Erica, you ain't gotta be so damn rude. Like Summer said, we were coming to check on y'all." Troy had the nerve to put his two cents in. He could kiss my ass, too.

"Listen, I ain't trying to be rude, but like I said, Shayla is trying to sleep. You guys are welcome to come back later. Thank y'all for the gift, we appreciate it," I said sincerely. I did appreciate everything they had been doing for us.

"Can I see my stepdaughter? You might as well get used to me because if she is Troy's, I will be around. I don't want any problems with you, so let's act like adults here." She came behind me and tried to pull the blanket from over Shayla's head, and I quickly moved away.

"I said get out! We don't wanna see anybody right now!" I yelled so loud, it woke Shayla, and she started crying.

"Ssshhh, baby, it's OK. Mama sorry." I tried to calm her down, but she wasn't having that. She screamed louder.

"Is everything all right in here?" Nurse Fannie rushed into the room, looking concerned.

"No, I asked you guys to hold my visitors, and they still managed to get in. So, no, everything is not all right. I want you to put them out of my room." I pointed to Troy and Summer. I wasn't in the mood.

"We won't be going anywhere until I see my daughter." Troy mugged the nurse, and Summer followed suit.

"Erica, you can't keep the father of your child from seeing her. I don't want to get in you all's business, so I'm going to leave. Let me know if you need anything else," she said just before she left out the room. At this point, I was tired of fighting, so I handed Shayla to Summer, and sat on the bed.

"Oh my God, she is beautiful!" Summer squealed. When she did, Shayla jumped.

"Thank you. I'm sorry, y'all, I'm just trying to protect Shayla. I don't want people laughing and talking about her because she is different," I apologized to them. Sitting down, Summer just stared at her, and I thought it was so cute.

"Erica, you don't have to worry about anyone talking about her. She is beautiful, and if she is Troy's, we are gonna have to get along for the kids' sake. I don't have anything against you, so hopefully, we can squash what we have going on." She sounded so sincere, and I felt the tears rolling down my face. Troy came over and hugged me, and it felt so good to be in a man's arm, even if he wasn't mine.

"Erica, chill out, man. You know we got you if you need anything." He hugged me tighter. Summer got up and handed Shayla to Troy, and he took her and sat down in the chair.

"I'm sorry if we got off on the wrong foot, but I hope we can stop all this childish mess. We are too grown for this. Even if Shayla is not Troy's, if you need anything, just call us." She stuck her hand out for me to shake. Instead of shaking it, I pulled her in for a hug. At first, I think she was just as shocked as I was but she finally hugged me back.

Letting her go, I wiped the tears from my eye. "My bad, I didn't mean to get my tears on you. I appreciate you guys for coming by. Since you are here, I got the DNA test back and thought we could open it together." I held up the manila envelope.

Troy looked up and nodded. Handing Shayla to me, I put her down in the bassinet. My hands were sweaty and shaky because I knew the truth before he had asked for the test. I wasn't ready for this to be over yet, so I stalled as long as I could. Excusing myself, I went to the restroom. While I was in there, I cried my eyes out. Once I had no more tears left to cry, I got up and got myself together. Exiting the bathroom, all eyes were on me. Walking over to the table, I picked up the envelope. Ripping it open, I skimmed over it, and it said that Troy was 99.9% the father. It shocked the hell out of me. I thought for sure she would be Shaq's, but I was happy that she was indeed Troy's.

"Well, congratulations, Troy, it says you are the father.

Now that she is yours, maybe y'all can bond more. I know this is a lot to take in, but here are the results." I handed them the results and Summer looked mad as hell. She might as well move over because we weren't going anywhere.

"We meant everything we said, and now that we know Troy is the daddy, we will be in Shayla's life." Summer came over and hugged me one last time, and Troy followed suit. I could tell he wasn't happy, but he would come around.

Walking over to the bassinet, Summer picked up Shayla and kissed her cheeks. That made my heart melt. After all I had put them through, they still loved my baby. Summer passed her to Troy, and he did the same thing. I knew he was a great father to the twins, and soon, they would need to meet their sister. I knew they would treat my baby like they did theirs, so I wasn't worried about that. I felt like a burden had been lifted off my shoulders. They stayed for a little longer and talked. It felt really good to talk to someone. They gave me a final hug and were out the door. Deciding I needed a nap, I called the nurse to get Shayla for a little while. Today had turned out to be a great day. No matter what anyone said about Summer, she was an all right person in my book.

I was awakened out of my sleep by the phone ringing. Reaching for it, I answered it, and it was Shaq's stupid ass. When he started talking, I almost hung up on his ass. We didn't need his ass; we were okay. I was going to make sure Shayla had everything she wanted and needed, and I was going to do it with or without him.

"Nice time for your ass to call. You got some nerve, nigga, but that's OK, we don't need you. Today, we found out that Shayla is Troy's, so I hope you have a happy life." I was pissed because for once, I was getting some good sleep, and his ass wanted to call with this bullshit.

"I'm glad I'm not the father. I didn't want anything to do with her anyway. Now that that's out of the way, leave me alone. Monica and I are trying to work things out."

"No problem. You didn't say nothing but a word. I know you will be back though because you can't resist me, so you can tell that lie to someone else. Your wish is my command, though." Shaq could kiss all my ass because I knew he would be back.

"Believe that shit if you want to. I have no kind of attachment to you now so you can kiss my ass. I hope you don't think Troy is gonna come running back to you. He already made it clear that he wasn't leaving Summer, so that baby you had for him was for nothing," he spat harshly.

"We already agreed, but why am I explaining myself to you? Nigga, there is nothing we have to talk about. Lose my damn number." I hung up on his ass. I wasn't wasting my breath talking to his ignorant ass. Fuck him.

Calling the nurses' station, I asked if they could bring my baby to me. I needed her at the moment. She was the only good thing to come out of this situation, and I was glad Shaq wasn't her father because he wasn't shit. I was going to teach her to never let a man run over her and to make sure she picked the right man to settle down with. When they brought her in, I hugged her tightly and kissed her all over her face. Tears started streaming down my face. She was so perfect, and I was going to make sure she had the best life possible.

Chapter 15

Shaq

When I finally called Erica back, and she told me I wasn't the father, a nigga was happy as shit. I could look at the baby and tell she wasn't mine, though. I knew that all kids came out differently, but when Ken came out, she looked just like a nigga. A nigga was walking around the room doing the dougie; she had just made my day.

Monica's ass had been acting up, and I didn't know what her problem was. Hell, she better be glad I still wanted her ass after the stunt she had pulled, but that was the past, and we were trying to move on from that. Every time she told me they were going over to her mother's house, I volunteered to take them. She could think again if she thought she was going to give her pussy up to another nigga. I had that shit on lock. I didn't know why she called herself in her feelings. I was trying to protect her ass, and this was how she repaid a nigga, by not giving me any pussy. We hadn't fucked in three weeks, and a nigga was backed up. I was tired of her acting like a brat. I needed some pussy, and she was about to give it to me willingly, or I was about to take it. When I walked into the room, she was laying on her stomach with her ass on display. I walked over to her and slapped her on the ass. She jumped and tried to get off the bed, but I was quicker than she was. I grabbed her and threw her on the bed.

"Calm yo' little ass down, and give me some of this sweet pussy." I ripped her boy shorts off.

"Please don't do this, Shaq." She had tears in her eyes, but those tears didn't mean shit to me.

"No need to cry now because Daddy is getting his pussy.

You have been holding out on me." I was now eye level with her pussy, and I flicked my tongue over it. She tasted so damn sweet. Covering her pussy lips with my mouth, I started eating her pussy. She moaned and squirmed, so I knew I was getting the job done.

"Please, Shaq, don't do this." She had tears running down her face, and at this point, I couldn't go through with it. Getting up from the bed, I left out the room and went to the bathroom to get myself together.

Looking in the mirror, I didn't know the person I saw. I needed to get myself together. I'd never had to rape anybody to get pussy. I needed a reality check. Washing my face and brushing my teeth, I looked and saw I needed a retwist. I had been letting myself go with all the shit that had been going on. Once I was done in the bathroom, I grabbed my phone and dialed Trina. Trina was a ghetto chick who lived beside my mother who I let retwist my hair from time to time. When she told me she would be over in an hour, I got myself together and headed to the living room. On the way to the living room, I heard sniffling. Peeking in the room Monica was in, I saw her balled up on the floor, crying. Seeing her crying like that tugged at a nigga's heart. Pushing the door open, I made my way over to her. Pulling her into my chest, I let her get it all out.

"I'm sorry, baby, I never meant to hurt you. I have been going through a lot of shit, and you aren't making it any better." I rubbed her back while she cried.

"Shaq, I can't be with you like that anymore. You hurt me, and I just can't look at you the same anymore." I looked into her eyes and saw the fear. I never wanted her to be scared of me, all I wanted to do was love her, and I couldn't even do that right. A nigga had fucked up. She pulled away from me and rushed out the room. Placing my head in my hands, a nigga was lost. Where did I go wrong?

Knocking on the door, she screamed, "Go away!" I was going to let her have that, but she wasn't going anywhere. Once all this shit blew over, me, her, and Ken were going to be a family. I didn't know where my mama had taken Ken, but I needed to hug my baby girl. If they weren't back soon, I would have to go looking for them.

Hearing the doorbell ring, I peeped out the hole and saw that it was Trina. Opening the door, I let her in. She still looked as good as I remembered. She had a little belly, but she was still beautiful. She was about 5'8, and 115 pounds soaking wet. I didn't know why she wore all that damn makeup because she was pretty without it. In my opinion, she looked like a damn clown with it on. She didn't have weave in her head, which surprised the fuck out of me. Looking at baby girl, she didn't look that bad. I might have to sample that pussy since Monica was playing. Moving out of the way, I let her in. She came in and started on my dreads. Sitting between her legs, the heat that radiated between them was hot as fuck.

"When you gonna stop playing with a nigga and let me fuck?"

"I am not about to play with your hoe ass, Shaq. When you get your life together, holla at me. Until then, I will be your hairstylist." She started popping her damn gum and that shit annoyed the hell out of me.

"Man, Trina, ain't nobody playing with you. I see how you be lusting for a nigga's dick. Stop playing and let me get the pussy. I promise I'll make it worth your while." I saw the wheels turning in her head like she was thinking about what I had just said.

"OK, but you better make it worth my while. If you gonna

play, I don't want it. Come on, I wanna see what that mouth do anyway," she smirked. She just didn't know I was about to have her ass climbing the walls.

She stood up and pulled her shorts down, and she didn't have any underwear on. She knew what she was doing. I knew I was wrong as hell because Monica was in the house, but oh well. I wasn't going to fuck her in the living room, though; that would be mad disrespectful to my mama. Picking up her clothes, I led her to the room I slept in. When we got in the room, she stood over in the corner, looking scared as hell and I had to laugh at her ass. She knew damn well she wasn't shy. I stood there, admiring her body and baby girl had a banging-ass body. From her ass to her perky breasts. My mouth started watering thinking about sucking her gumdrops.

Walking over to her, I pushed her on the bed, and she spread her legs wide open. She had to be ready the way her pussy glistened. Bending down, getting close to her pussy, I sniffed it. If the pussy wasn't clean, I wasn't going to put it in my mouth. Her shit smelled like cinnamon, and I loved that sweet shit. I took her pussy into my mouth, and she started squirming, and I hadn't even started yet. Licking her slowly, she started moaning. The way she was moaning sent me into overdrive. Alternating between licking and sucking, she went crazy. Next thing I knew, she was wetting my face up. I wasn't about to let any of that sweet shit go to waste, so I licked her dry. She was laying there, breathing hard. At this point, my dick was harder than a motherfucker. Releasing my monster, I laid down on the bed.

"Come sit on this dick." I stroked my dick up and down. She got up, and I saw the lust in her eyes. She could suck the dick if she wanted to. Dropping to her knees, she started sucking my dick like her life depended on it.

"Fuck, daddy, he's so big." She took my dick out of her mouth and started talking to my dick.

Placing it back into her mouth, she started bobbing her head up and down. Her head game was the truth. Shit, it was the best head I had gotten in a long time. The warmth of her mouth had a nigga's head gone. Fucking her face a little longer, I came hard as fuck in her mouth. Like the nasty bitch she was, she swallowed, causing my dick to get hard again. She came and straddled me and placed my dick into her dripping wet pussy and I almost lost control. Her pussy was wet as fuck. I had to focus on something else because if not, I would cum deep inside her walls.

Bouncing her ass up and down, I was enjoying myself. She was going buck wild on the dick. She started slow grinding, and I placed one of her gumdrops into my mouth and sucking on them had her going crazy. Next thing I knew, her body started jerking, and she rode the wave out. Flipping her over, I started dicking her down from the back. Her ass bounced, and that shit drove me crazy. One more deep stroke and I pulled out and came all over her back. That pussy was the truth. I was going to have to dip in that more often.

She laid there while I got up and went to the bathroom to clean up. Once I cleaned my dick off, I looked at the room door that Monica was in and shook my head. If she weren't going to give it to me, I would get it from somewhere else. Making it back in the room, Trina was on her side, snoring lightly. That dick had put her to sleep. Opening her legs, I cleaned her up. Pulling the cover over her body, I left out the room to get something to eat. A nigga was hungry as fuck.

Heading to the kitchen, Monica came out the room, and I knew she was about to start some shit. As I walked to the kitchen, she was on my heels, but I wasn't about to feed into her bullshit, though. If she wanted to leave, her ass was free to go, but she wasn't about to take my daughter, so she could get that out of her head.

"Shaq, your ass is so damn disrespectful. How the fuck are you gonna be fucking another bitch while I'm in the other room?" She hit me in the back. I would be dead ass wrong if I turned around and hit her ass back.

"Keep yo' damn hands off me before I hit your ass back." I turned around and gave her a death stare.

"Fuck you, nigga. I wish you would. Don't worry, my daughter and I will be gone as soon as your mama comes back. I'm too good for the shit I put up with." When she said that, all hell broke loose. There was no way in hell she was going to take my daughter away from me. No matter what we went through, I was a good father.

"Gone on somewhere with that shit. You ain't taking my daughter no-fucking-where. You can go, but my daughter is staying here."

"Nope, if I leave, she is leaving with me. I won't leave her here with your no-good ass." She was all in my ear, screaming and shit. I wasn't even hungry anymore.

Making my way into the living room, I sat down on the chair and turned the TV on. Monica was still talking, but I tuned her ass out. At this point, we had nothing else to talk about. I had said what I had to say, so I was about to go out and get some air. I needed to go by the trap and re-up anyway. If Monica thought she was taking my daughter from me, she had another thing coming.

Trina was just getting up, and her damn hair was all over the place, but she was beautiful, no doubt.

"Hey, ma, I need to make a run, but you are welcome to stay here while I'm gone."

She frowned at me. "Naw, I can go home. You can get up with me later. I'm not about to stay here while you are not here." She was now getting up, putting her clothes on, and just like that, she was out the door.

Getting myself together, I exited the house and jumped in my car. A nigga's mind was all over the place. I was never one who had to rape a bitch to get pussy. I knew I had hurt Monica, but I didn't mean that shit, I just wanted to get my rocks off. I cranked the car up and made it out of my mother's driveway, and it took me no time to get to the trap on Connell St. Word on the street was that Trent was murdered over some pussy. Before everything went down, I had told him to leave Carla alone. Her ass wasn't anything but trouble. I guess he had to find out the hard way. That nigga was wild.

Pulling up to the block, I chopped it up with Tim for a minute. Tim was the nigga who had taken over when Trent was killed. Making my way into the house, I got some more weed and was out the door. I didn't need to stay over there long. Hell, I was thinking about giving this shit up. I had to do better for my daughter.

Getting back in my ride, I pulled off and headed to get something to eat. Erica popped up into a nigga's mind, but I pushed her to the back of my mind. I wasn't fucking with her ass like that anymore.

Getting me something to eat at Taco Bell, I made my way back to the crib, and it took me a little over fifteen minutes to get there. Once I made it, I sat in the car, eating my tacos. Them bitches were on point. After I was done, I exited the ride. When I got in the house, it was quiet as shit.

It was weird my mama wasn't home yet, and she hadn't called, either. I knew something was up, I just hoped they were OK. Closing and locking the door, I headed to the kitchen. On the counter, there was a piece of paper with my name on it. This was some middle school shit. Who the hell still wrote notes? Grabbing the letter, I opened it. Monica was on one.

Shaq, I'm sorry I couldn't be the woman you needed. I will not allow you to treat me the way you do. I have tried to be the best woman I could be for you, but my best still ain't enough for you. You have disrespected me one time too many and I will not allow my daughter to grow up thinking it is OK for a man to do her wrong. She deserves so much better than you. I wished I would have gone the other way when I first met you, but that was my mistake. I hope and pray you find someone to be the woman you need. I took a lot of shit from you, but I am so tired of you treating me like I ain't shit. I love you, but I love me more. My daughter and I will see you when you get your shit together. She doesn't need to be around you with the way you are. Please don't come looking for us; we are better off without you. Have a good life! Monica.

I swear when I read that letter, I was hurt. How the fuck could Monica take my daughter away from me? With all the shit we had been going through, I had never brought my daughter in it. Balling the letter up, I threw it into the trash. I needed to get my shit together if I ever wanted to see my daughter again. Grabbing a bottle of water out the fridge, I turned it up. Making my way to the bathroom, I just couldn't believe she was doing this shit. Who was I kidding? I knew she was going to get tired of my shit sooner or later, I just didn't think it would be this soon.

Once I got into the bathroom, I turned the water on and waited for it to get to the right temperature. Stripping out of my clothes, I stepped into the shower. While I was in the shower, I thought about all the things I had been through in life. I'd had one hell of a life, but things must go on. Washing and rinsing a couple of times, I got out of the shower. Placing the towel around me, I proceeded to brush my teeth. Looking in the mirror, I looked like death. Feeling satisfied, I walked out the bathroom and was met by a gun pointing in my face. Damn, this couldn't be the end of my life.

Chapter 16

Monica

It hurt me to leave Shaq, but I was tired of his bullshit. After all the shit I had put up with his ass, he still treated me like shit. My daughter and I deserved so much more. When he left to go wherever he was going, I packed me and my daughter's stuff, and when his mama brought her home, we were going to be out the door. I wasn't sure where we were going yet, but I needed to get as far away from him as I could. I was an emotional wreck. While I packed, I cried. I needed someone to lean on, but I didn't have a soul. Grabbing my phone, I dialed Craig to see if he could meet me somewhere. I knew we weren't on talking terms, but I was going to push my luck, and he wasted no time answering.

"You good, ma? What's going on?" He sounded worried.

"No, I'm not OK. I'm a fucking wreck, and I need you right now," I told him in between cries.

"Where the fuck are you? I can come to you. Did that nigga put his hands on you? I swear I'ma kill him with my bare hands." The way he said it made me laugh.

"What the fuck you laughing at? I'm dead serious."

"I'm fine, but I can't talk right now. I'm packing me and my daughter's stuff. We are leaving. Can you meet me somewhere?" I needed him right now.

"Yeah, tell me the place, and I'm there. You know I got you, right?" I knew without a doubt he had my back, just like I had his.

"I know, but meet me at Holiday Inn on Peach Street. I'll

text you once I get there." The line went dead, so I knew he had hung up. Taking our bags to the car, I came back in and waited for them to return.

Thirty minutes later, Louise finally came back with my baby, and I didn't even give her a chance to put her down. I snatched my baby from her arms and headed to the car. I made sure to buckle her in and kissed her cheeks. Once I had her settled in, I got in and headed to the Holiday Inn. On the ride there, I called Craig to let him know I was on my way. When we made it there, Craig was standing outside, waiting for us. He made it to the car, pulled me out and kissed my forehead. It felt so good to be wrapped up in his arms.

"Talk to me, what's going on? Trouble in paradise?" He gave me a death stare. The way he stared at me made me uncomfortable.

"Something like that. I had to get my daughter and me away from his ass. I feel so lost now. I don't have anywhere for us to go." I fell into his arms and cried.

"Calm down, baby. You and little mama can stay with me. I have enough room for y'all. Save your money, and we can go look for y'all somewhere to stay. Don't worry about Shaq; we going to get his ass." I appreciated Craig for wanting to help us, but I didn't want that. I wanted to do this on my own.

"Thank you, but no thank you. We will be staying here until tomorrow, and then we will go house hunting." He mean mugged me.

"Monica, stop being so damn stubborn and let me help you." He walked up to me and kissed me, and that kiss made my knees weak. I was going to see where this went.

"OK, we will stay with you, but first thing in the morning, we will be leaving."

"Follow me to my house so we can get little mama in the bed." He was so damn thoughtful.

"Lead the way, daddy." I was willing to let him take care of me.

On the way over, I was nervous as hell because I wasn't ready to take it to the next level with Craig. I appreciated everything he wanted to do for me, but I felt like I need to do this alone. Before we made it to Craig's house, Ken started crying, and I knew she was probably hungry. Calling Craig, I told him I needed to get Ken something to eat before we went there. He told me it was cool and that he was going to stop by the 7-11 up the road, and he would meet me there. Stopping by McDonald's, I ordered Ken a chicken nugget kids meal. When I got to Craig's house, I would whip us up something. Paying and receiving the food, we left. Getting to 7-11, I spotted Craig's midnight black Charger parked on the side, so I pulled behind him and flashed my lights. Getting out, he made his way over to the car.

"What's up, baby? Y'all ready?" he asked as he licked his lips.

"Can you go to the store and get me some Hot Cheetos and a large blueberry slush, please?" I poked my lips out.

"You know I got you. Does little mama need anything?" he asked, looking in the backseat at Ken, who was giving her chicken nuggets hell.

"You can get her some cheese puffs and an apple juice. That will be all. Thank you." I kissed him on the cheek.

Wasting no time, he made his way inside. While he was inside, I checked my phone. As I expected, Shaq had been blowing me up. I knew he wasn't going to stop, so I blocked his ass all together. I knew it was selfish, but I meant what I said. Until he got his shit together, he wasn't going to see Ken. He could hang it up with me; I could never be with him like that again. While I was with Shaq, I was never happy. I knew my worth as a woman, and I deserved so much better. Hell, if you asked me, Ken did, too. Looking back at my baby, she was knocked out. I knew that once I bathed her, she would sleep through the night and that would give me some time to get to know Craig. He seemed like a genuine person.

He made his way out to the car and handed me the stuff. Sticking the straw in the cup, I took a sip of my slushy, and it was good as hell. I drunk too much and got a damn brain freeze. Heading back over to his car, we were on the way to his house. Once we made it there, I popped my trunk and opened the back door to get Ken out. Her grandma must have tired her out because she would wake up and go right back to sleep. Craig went to the trunk, got our bags out and led us to the house. When we entered the house, it was nice as hell. The furniture was cream and black, and I instantly fell in love.

"Where can I lay her down?" I asked.

"Oh, shit, my bad. You can follow me to the guest room. I'm being all rude and shit," he laughed, leading me up the hall. When we made it to the room, I laid Ken on the bed, and my damn arm had fallen asleep.

"When you're done with her, you can come tend to me," he said just as he left out the room. His ass thought he was slick. Once Ken was settled in, I made my way to the living room.

"Make yourself at home," he told me as he walked off. I was in dire need of a bath.

"Can I take a shower somewhere? My body needs it." I just wanted to soak.

"You can go in the bathroom in the hall, or you can come in the bathroom in my room," he smirked. His ass wasn't slick.

"I'll take the one in the hall, just in case Ken wakes up." I started getting my clothes out and made my way to the bathroom.

Turning the water on, I waited for the tub to fill up. Putting a little bubble bath in, I stripped down to my birthday suit, and when I got in, the temperature was just right, and the water relaxed my body. Sitting in the tub, I let my head fall back. Today had been a hell of a day, and hopefully, it would be a better night. I must have fallen asleep because Craig came in and woke me up, and the water was cold as shit. Washing and rinsing quickly, I got out. Drying off, I put my clothes on and lotioned my body. Once I was done, I peeped in the room and checked on Ken, and she looked like she was sleeping so peacefully, and I was going to be on the other side of her in a minute. I was tired as hell.

When I made it back in the living room, Craig was stretched out on the chair. He had his eyes closed, and I thought he was sleep. I was about to make my way into the room with Ken when he sat up.

"Come sit and talk to me. I ain't gonna bite unless you want me to." The way he said it had my other set of lips responding.

"I thought you were sleep, so I was about to go get in the bed with Ken." I made my way back over to the couch and threw my legs over his.

"Naw, I wasn't sleeping, just resting my eyes. It took your ass long enough, I almost fell asleep," he laughed.

"You so silly. I didn't realize I was asleep until you woke me up. I must have been tired. It has been a long day, you know?" I hit him with the pillow.

"So, tell me what this is?" He pointed from me to him. I was confused; I didn't know what we were as of yet.

I shrugged. "I really don't know what this is. What do you want?" I turned the question around on him.

"I want this, but only when you are ready to give it to me." He pointed to my heart. I blushed. He knew what to say to me.

"I want this, too, just not now. Let's just take it slow and see where it goes." It was a start. I didn't want to jump out of one relationship and get into another one without thinking it out. Hell, who was to say I was over Shaq? I still needed closure. I ended things with a letter, but I didn't let him explain. Who was I fooling? We had been over for a while, but I hoped that he got his shit together for Ken, though.

"I'm good with that. Whatever you wanna do, I'm down for the ride." I could see myself with him. He seemed real and true, and that was what I needed. As of right now, I was just going to focus on Ken, and getting my life together. If it were meant to be, then it would be.

"You hungry, because I'm starving. I could hook us up something if you want." My damn stomach was touching my damn back. I just hoped he had something simple and quick I could cook.

Nodding, he got up, and I followed suit. When we made it to the kitchen, I started checking to see what he had. For a man, his kitchen was fully stocked. Deciding to cook something simple, I took the chicken breast out and put them in the sink to thaw out. While I was getting stuff together to make us a snack, Craig sat at the table, staring at me and I blushed. I was going to make chicken alfredo since that was simple. It was almost eleven at night, and I was about to make pasta.

While the chicken thawed, Craig and I continued talking. He was an amazing man. It was crazy what this man was doing to me. I just hoped I was strong enough to keep my legs closed tonight. Just when I was about to get the pasta started, I heard Ken crying. Rushing into the room, I picked her up. She was probably scared because we were in an unfamiliar place.

"Ssshhh, Mama got you. What's wrong with Mama's baby?" I cooed.

"Mama, pee-pee," she told me. Rushing to the bathroom, I placed her on the toilet. Once she was done, I helped her wipe and washed her hands.

"You ready to take a bath?" I asked her, and she nodded.

Going over to the tub, I ran a bubble bath. While the water was running, I went into the room and got her some night clothes to put on. Making it back to the bathroom, I started undressing her and placed her in the tub. She loved taking baths, mainly because she could play in the water. I let her play for a little while, and once she was done, I bathed her and took her out. Wrapping the towel around her, I took her in the room and lotioned her body. Once we were all finished, we headed back into the kitchen where Craig was, and he had the kitchen smelling good. If you looked at him, you wouldn't think he could cook. My stomach instantly started growling. Placing Ken on the floor, I made my way over to the stove to see if I could help him with anything. From the looks of things, he was almost finished. He told Ken and me to have a seat at the table, and he would fix us a plate. Wasting no time, I sat Ken down and sat beside her.

"You ready to eat, Ken?"

She started clapping her little hands. "Eat-eat, mama." She was going crazy in the chair.

Craig walked over and placed a little saucer in front of her, and she smiled at him. That warmed my heart. Ken picked up her fork and started eating. Ken wasn't shy at all; if it was time to eat, she was eating. He then walked over to me and placed a plate in front of me. It looked and smelled so good. I said a quick prayer and dug in. Craig gave Ken some apple juice, and me, a bottle of water. Once he took care of us, he placed his plate down next to me and started eating. It was so damn good. I don't know, I might have to keep him. He was sexy, and he could cook.

Once we were finished, I placed the dishes in the sink. Once Ken was asleep, I would wash them. Straightening up the kitchen, we made our way into the living room. When we got in there, I placed Ken in my lap and turned the TV on. Craig sat beside us and put his arm around me. Pulling me in close to him, I was content. We decided to put *SpongeBob SquarePants* on for Ken. She didn't last any time. It wasn't even ten minutes later, and she was out for the count. Hell, I wasn't far behind her. Picking her up, I took her into the room and laid her down on the bed. Tucking her in, I went back into the living room with Craig. When I started to sit down, he pulled me into his lap, and I didn't object. Laying my head back, getting comfortable, I felt his manhood rise. I moved away from him and sat next to him.

"I know you ain't scared of this." He pointed to his fully erect penis. From the looks of things, he was working with a monster.

"Naw, why should I be scared? I know that once we reach that point, you will take your time with me."

"You damn right. You won't ever have to worry about anything. Whatever you need, I got you." He winked at me. I wasn't ready for what he had to offer me yet.

"OK, well, I'm going to bed. We will talk in the morning." I got up and made my way to the room that Ken was in. I pulled her close to me, and just that quick, I was out for the count.

Chapter 17

Craig

I didn't know why Monica was playing. I could see she wanted me just as badly as I wanted her. Fucking with her would have a nigga with blue balls, but I wasn't in a rush, though. I would wait however long she made me. She was worth it. I just couldn't believe Shaq had fucked up, but I was kinda glad he had, though. She wasn't going anywhere anytime soon.

Getting out the chair, I was going to bed. Hell, Monica had left me, so that was my cue to go to bed. On the way to my room, I peeked in the room where Monica and her daughter were sleeping, and they looked like they were sleeping so peacefully. I pulled the door and proceeded to my room. Once inside, I went to take a piss and wash my ass. I understood where she was coming from, though. I was going to wait for her, but I didn't say I wasn't going to be getting other pussy because I was. Hell, she wasn't giving it up, and I had needs, too. Turning the shower on, I waited for it to get as hot as it could. The steam relaxed a nigga. Stepping in, I let the water run over my body. While I was in there, I started thinking about Monica's ass. Fifteen minutes had passed, and I felt a cold breeze. Peeking my head out the side of the curtain, I saw Monica standing there, looking sexy as hell. She was butt naked, and I had to pinch myself to make sure I wasn't dreaming. As I thought, it was Monica in the flesh. Opening the shower curtain, she eased in.

"Damn, ma, you sexy as fuck." I had to wipe the slobber from my mouth. She had a nigga drooling and shit, but I didn't want her to do anything she would later regret. I wanted it to be special.

"Ssshhhh, I know I said I wasn't ready, but I want you right now," she moaned.

Her wish was my command. Wasting no time, I had her ass pinned on the wall. I was a pussy eater, so it was only right for me to please her pussy first. Dropping to my knees, she placed her legs around my neck, and her pussy smelled so damn sweet. I was about to demolish it. Putting my lips over her pussy, I started licking her slowly. She was wet as fuck, and between the water and her pussy, a nigga was drowning. The way she moaned drove a nigga crazy. Sucking and slurping, I was fucking it up. Feeling her body jerk, I knew she was cumming. I made sure not to waste any, and when I was satisfied, I placed her on her feet. The water was cold, and I wanted to fuck her in the bed. Getting out the tub, I gave her a towel to dry off, and I did the same. Wasting no time, I gently laid her on the bed. I could see so much lust in her eyes, but I wanted to make sure she was ready for what I was about to give her.

"You sure you ready for this? You know you don't have to do anything you don't want to do."

"Yes, please give it to me, baby. Just don't hurt me." I didn't plan on hurting her, I just wanted to love her.

Grabbing a condom from my drawer, I placed it over all nine inches. When Monica saw my dick, her eyes almost popped out of her head. Yeah, I was about to be in this pussy all night, I just hoped she was ready. Lining my dick up with her pussy, I pushed it in, inch by inch. When I first entered her, she flinched. Telling her to relax, I slowly started fucking her. Her damn pussy was so damn gushy, I had to focus on something else. When I got myself together, I started giving her long, deep strokes. To say that her pussy was good was a damn understatement. Her pussy was bomb as fuck.

"Fuck, daddy. Oh my God, I love this dick. Please fuck me," she moaned.

She didn't have to tell me twice; I started fucking it up. The deeper I went, the wetter she got, and it had a nigga feeling like a straight bitch. I knew I wasn't going to last in this pussy; it was too damn good.

"Damn, girl, why your pussy so damn wet?" I moaned against her neck.

She started grinding her hips under me, and I went deeper. The deeper I went, the louder she moaned. I had to put my hand over her mouth because I didn't want to wake little mama up. She didn't seem to care about that, though, as she bit my damn hand. I snatched it away from her mouth. I guess that was what I got for trying to keep her quiet. I started fucking her harder, and the next thing I knew, she was cumming, and I wasn't far behind her. Cumming in the condom, I collapsed on her, but I wasn't finished with her yet. Taking the condom off, I went and flushed it down the toilet. Grabbing another one, I rolled it on my dick. Diving back in, I placed her leg on my shoulder, making that pussy talk to me, just how I liked it. Flipping her over, I made her arch her back. Once it was just how I wanted it, I started pounding her pussy, and I heard her gasp for air. She didn't see it coming as I rammed it all the way into her pussy.

"Damn, daddy, fuck me harder!" she screamed.

Goddamn, I was trying to show her mercy, but she wanted it rough, and I was going to give it to her. Grabbing a fistful of her hair, I pulled it, and that sent her into overdrive as she started bouncing her ass on my dick. I was enjoying the view. I liked to be in control, so I flipped her back over on her back, grabbed her neck and started choking her. I wasn't squeezing her neck hard, just enough to make that pussy cum. Monica's ass was a freak, and I loved that shit. Little did she know, she wasn't going anywhere. We were going to make this shit work. She was going to have me killing niggas just because they looked at her wrong. Once she got her nut out the way, I filled the condom up. I rolled off her and fell on the opposite side of the bed.

"Shit, girl, you know that's my pussy, right?" I asked, tapping her pussy. Her shit was going to make a nigga lose it.

"You know that goes both ways. If this is your pussy, that's my dick. Show me the same respect, and we are good." She thought she was getting something straight.

"Come on, let's take a shower. We have a long day, and it's already three."

She rolled off the bed and limped to the bathroom, and I laughed at a job well down. Once we got to the bathroom, I turned the shower on, and we stepped in. She made sure to keep her distance from me. If she moved the wrong way, I was going to dip back in it. I laughed at her ass, but I wasn't going to mess with her, though. I got the rag and started washing my body, and Monica did the same. She took my washcloth from me and washed my back. A nigga wasn't used to shit like this, so it threw me a little. She handed me her washcloth, and I did the same for her. Once we were clean, we hopped out the shower. Drying off, we made our way back to the room, and I stripped the bed; there was no way in hell I was going to sleep in a bed full of nut. Walking over to the closet, I grabbed some fresh sheets, placing them on the bed. Monica got in, and I laid behind her, pulling her close to me. I could get used to this. Dozing off, I was awakened out of my sleep by my cell phone going off. I just laid there. I thought they would get the hint, but they called back. Getting irritated, I snatched my phone off the nightstand and looked at the caller ID, and it was Troy. It had to be important for him to be calling this early.

"Nigga, this better be important since you calling me this early." Usually, he wouldn't call me this early. I still had my eyes closed, thinking that maybe once the call was over, I could go back to sleep.

"Nigga, shut yo' ass up and meet us at the warehouse. We got a little problem." That was all he had to say, and just that quick, I was wide awake.

"Bet. Let me throw on some clothes, and I'm on the way." The line went dead.

Placing the phone on the nightstand, I started moving around, careful not to wake Monica. She was sleeping so peacefully, and she looked so beautiful. I couldn't believe she was all mine. Walking over to the closet, I started getting dressed. Pulling out my black jeans and a black thermal shirt, I was ready for war. Grabbing my hoody, I kissed Monica on the forehead, and I was out. Before I left, I checked in on little mama, and she was knocked the fuck out, stretched all over the bed. I just laughed. Walking into the room, I placed the cover on her. Leaving out the room, I left the door cracked. Grabbing my keys, I set the alarm, and I was out. The drive over to the warehouse was short. Getting there, I parked my car and headed to the warehouse. Inside, Sam and Troy were posted up on the wall.

"It took yo' ass long enough. Now, since you're here, we can get down to business," Troy started.

"OK, I'm all ears. What's up?" I sat on the couch.

"We have a plan to bring Shaq to us." I was interested in

how we were going to get him.

"We are gonna kidnap his mama, and if she cooperates, she will be able to walk free. We won't hurt her unless she gives us a reason to." Sam started going over the plan. This sounded like a plan, and I was in.

"OK, so how exactly are we gonna get her?"

"We have been following her for a minute, and her route is the same. We take her from the store, bring her here, and we go from there. If she gives us the information, she can walk," Troy stated certainly.

"Cool, count me in. Couldn't this wait until daybreak, though? A nigga is tired as hell." I mugged them niggas, and they shook their heads. These were my niggas, and whatever they needed, I had their backs, but all I could think about right now was laying under Monica's fine ass. Dapping them up, I rolled out.

Chapter 18

Sam

Carla and I were finally at a happy place in life. She was starting to open up to me more, and I loved that shit. Life couldn't get any better. Carla was the missing piece to my puzzle. When I was in the streets, and I came home, Carla was my happy place. Things were finally starting to look up for a nigga. We were laying on the couch, watching TV. Well, I was anyway. Carla's ass had fallen asleep on a movie she had picked out. What kind of shit was that? I agreed to watch a Lifetime movie with her, and she fell asleep. Taking the remote, I turned to SportsCenter. Looking down at Carla, she was perfect. I moved her hair out of her face and laughed. Her ass was drooling on my damn leg, but that didn't bother me, though.

Picking her up bridal style, I carried her into the bedroom and laid her down. She stirred in her sleep a little, but not enough to wake up. After I laid her down, I stood by the side of the bed and just stared at her. She was a nigga's rib. We had only been together a little over a year, and I already wanted to pop the question. There was no time limit to love; if it was there, it was there.

Making my way to the bathroom, I turned the shower on. While the water got hot, I took a piss and washed my hands. Looking in the mirror, I saw a completely different nigga. If somebody had told me six years ago this would be my life, I would have laughed at their ass. I was happy, though. Hopping my ass in the shower, I wasted no time washing my ass. Once I was done, I dried off and threw on some boxers. I got in the bed, pulled Carla close to me, kissed her on the neck and told her I loved her. She mumbled it back, and that was the last thing I heard before

I was out. A nigga didn't know I was that tired until I had fallen asleep.

Waking up, 1 looked to my left and Carla wasn't there. I eased out the bed to wash my face and brush my teeth. Once I was satisfied, I followed the smell of food. When I got to the kitchen, Carla was standing over the stove with a thong and panty set on. She was beautiful, the way her skin glowed. Walking up behind her, I snaked my arms around her waist, and she smelled good enough to eat. Her scent drove a nigga crazy.

"Hey, baby!" She turned around and kissed me on the lips.

"Sup, bae? What you in here cooking? It smells good as shit in here." I kissed her one more time and backed up.

"Nachos. I had a craving for some," she told me, and I looked at her ass sideways. Only pregnant people had cravings. Come to think of it, she hadn't had her period this month. Yeah, a nigga was keeping up with her period.

"Baby, is there something you need to tell me?" I waited for her to respond. She was standing over by the stove with a silly grin on her face, and I knew without a doubt what it was.

"Baby, I don't know, but I'm two weeks late." She looked nervous as shit. Walking up to her, I picked her up and hugged her tight. She was about to make me the happiest man in the world.

"Why you look so nervous, baby? You know I got you, right?" I picked up her chin and kissed her lips.

"I know, baby, but what if I turn out like my mama? I don't know anything about raising a child." The tears started rolling down her face, and that shit broke a nigga's heart.

"You could never be your mother. If you are pregnant, we will learn together. I don't know shit about a baby, but I'm willing to learn. I don't want you worrying about anything; I got y'all." I placed my hands on her flat stomach.

"I went and bought a test the other day, but I haven't taken it yet. You wanna do it together?" she asked, walking over to me and kissing my lips. I snaked my tongue in her mouth, and the kiss got heated. Had a nigga wanting to bend her ass over the kitchen table, but right now wasn't the time.

"I wouldn't have it no other way. Let's go check, baby." Turning the food off and placing a lid on it, I picked her up and carried her to the bathroom.

When we got there, I put her down, and she went and got the test. She closed the lid on the toilet and sat down, reading the directions, and I stood there, just staring at her. Once she was done reading the instructions, she lifted the toilet seat and peed on the stick. I watched her like a hawk, and once she was done, she washed her hands. She told me we had to wait five minutes for the results, so I ran and got my phone; I didn't want to miss anything. Setting my alarm, we stood by the door, waiting. The anticipation was killing a nigga, and I almost peeked at it before the time was up, but I waited. As soon as the time was up, I ran over to the test and was confused as fuck. I saw two lines but wasn't sure what it meant. I held the test up, and tears rolled down Carla's face, and that was all I needed to see. They were happy tears.

"I guess you about to be a daddy," she told me as the tears flowed down her face.

"Fuck, you just made a nigga happy as shit. Damn, I can't believe this shit. I'm about to be a daddy." I pulled her to me and kissed her.

"I take it you are happy."

"Baby, I'm more than happy, I'm ecstatic!" I damn near screamed. "I would be happier if you make me the happiest man and marry a nigga." I dropped to my knees and grabbed her hand. I didn't have a ring yet, but she didn't have to worry about that; she could pick out whatever she wanted.

"Yesss, baby, I will marry you," she squealed, and I picked her up and hugged her tight.

I was the happiest man on earth. I had my baby, and she was having my baby. Walking her over to the bed, I laid her down gently. I was about to make love to my fiancée. Spreading her legs, my mouth started watering looking at her pussy. I was about to please my baby. Bending down, I placed my lips on her pussy. Flicking my tongue over her pearl, she started moaning and pulling my dreads. Pulling her ass close to me, I sucked on her pussy. She was always wet for a nigga, so I didn't have to do much.

"Fuck, baby, I'm cumm—" That was all she was able to get out before her body started jerking and her face twisted up. I loved that shit.

"That's right, baby. Let that shit go," I coached her, and made sure not to waste any of her sweet nectar.

Once she was done, I pulled my pants down and freed my dick. I was hard as steel by now. Stroking my dick, I tongued her down. That was one thing about her, she loved to taste herself. Coming up for air, I placed my dick at her opening. Once I was all the way in, I started fucking her slowly. Now that I knew she was pregnant, I could feel the difference; her shit was gushy as fuck. I stopped fucking her and just stood there, looking at her. She contracted her walls around my dick, and I almost lost it. Climbing out of her, I laid on the bed and had her climb on the dick. She wasted no time, and once she adjusted to my length, she started fucking it up. Carla was a freaky bitch, *my* freaky bitch.

Bouncing up and down on my dick, she started playing with her nipples, and I just laid back and enjoyed the show. I started fucking her back, and she went harder. Goddamn, she was wetting my dick up, and I loved it. Her body began jerking, and she rode it out. Climbing off my dick, she tooted her ass up. She knew how I liked it. I could never get tired of her pussy; it was just so damn good. Thrusting inside of her, I grabbed a fistful of hair and almost forgot she was pregnant as I started fucking the shit out of her. She was matching my strokes, throwing her ass back. Not able to last any longer, I shot my seeds deep inside her wall and Carla fell on the bed, and I fell on the other side of her.

"Damn, baby, I love you so much." I kissed her lips.

"We love you, too, daddy." She was about to start some shit. She knew I liked when she called me daddy.

"Say daddy again." I started toying with her pearl.

"Ooohhh, daddy!" she moaned, and that shit made my dick stand to attention.

"Come fuck your dick, baby."

She climbed on the dick and started riding it like a rodeo, not missing a beat. This pussy was going to be the death of me, but I would deal with that when it came up. Right now, I was about to enjoy the show. Sweat rolled off her forehead, and she wiped it with the back of her hand, but that didn't stop her, though. She kept riding the dick, grinding my shit slowly, and I felt my nut rising. Tapping her ass, she came all over my dick, and I followed suit. She fell on my chest, panting hard as shit.

"You good, baby?" I asked, and she nodded.

"I need a shower. I'm all sticky and shit." She balled up her pretty face.

"I love you, sticky and all." I kissed her on the forehead.

Getting up from the bed, I pulled her up with me. When we made it to the bathroom, I turned the shower on. Once it was at the right temperature, we stepped in. Grabbing her loofah, I started washing her body down. That was one thing I loved about her. She let me take full control of her mind, body, and soul. Once I was done with her, she did the same for me. When she got to my dick, he started rising. I couldn't get enough of her ass.

"Down boy," I told my dick, and Carla fell out laughing.

"You so silly, baby. Come on, let's get out. I'm hungry and sleepy." Hell, I was hungry, too. Turning the water off, we climbed out. Drying each other off, we headed to the kitchen to eat. When we got there, I heard my phone vibrating, and I thought that whoever was calling would get the hint and hang up, but it kept ringing. Reaching it, I looked at it, and it was Troy.

"Talk to me, nigga," I answered.

"Damn, nigga, what the fuck are you doing? I done called your ass about fifty damn times." Looking at the call log, he wasn't lying. This had to be important.

"What's up, man? Is everything OK?" I grabbed a nacho off Carla's plate and stuck it in my mouth, and she took her plate and moved away from me.

"We have a situation. Meet me at the warehouse in fifteen minutes," he told me just as he hung up.

"Baby, I need to meet Troy, but I shouldn't be long. You wanna go over there till I come back?" I asked, and she licked her fingers. Ol' greedy ass. I had to laugh at her.

"Yeah, I need to go over and tell her the good news, and I need to see my babies," she told me as she got up and placed her plate in the sink.

Getting dressed, my mind was all over the place as I wondered what in the hell was going on. Once we were dressed, we were out the door. The drive over to Troy's and Summer's house was quiet. Carla was sitting on the passenger side, looking out the window. She seemed like she was deep in thought. Placing my hand on her thigh, I squeezed it. She looked at me and blew me a kiss. Little shit like that kept me sane. She was a nigga's backbone, and I couldn't wait until we said I do. When we got there, I leaned over and kissed Carla like it was my last day on Earth. Once we were finished, we said we loved each other, and she climbed out the car and headed for the door. Once she was inside, I peeled off.

Chapter 19

Carla

"Hey, sister, how are you?" I walked into the house and hugged her. She looked tired as hell. *Hell, I would be too if I'd just had twins*, I thought.

"Girl, I'm tired as hell. Don't get me wrong, I love being a mother, but sometimes, I get overwhelmed."

"I know, sis. Why don't you call me? You know I would come over and help you." I frowned at her, but I knew how Summer was. She was stubborn and thought she was Superman.

"I know, I just didn't wanna bother you." I wanted to slap her ass. That was what I was here for. We were family.

"Bitch, I ought to slap your ass. You wouldn't be bothering me, we are family," I told her and left to go get Tay out her swing. She was getting fat as hell. She was so little when she was born, but not anymore. I didn't know what Summer had been feeding her ass.

"Hey, Tee Tee's baby," I cooed, and she looked at me and blew bubbles. I couldn't wait until I had my baby. "Where is Jr.?" I asked Summer.

"Girl, his fat butt in the bed. One is always asleep, and the other is up. They never sleep on the same shift," she told me just before she walked off to go check on him

Walking over to the chair, I placed Tay in my lap as I turned the TV on. She was a calm baby. Flipping through the channels, I stopped at *SpongeBob SquarePants*. Tay started kicking her hands and feet. She loved any cartoon, but SpongeBob was her favorite. Summer came back out holding Jr. in her arms, and damn, his ass was big as hell. She took Tay from me and handed me Jr.

"Damn, girl, what are you feeding these kids? They are big as hell. I don't remember them being this big." I bounced him on my leg.

"Girl, breast milk, that's it. They just greedy as hell," she laughed as she walked off to go change Tay.

Sitting down, playing with Jr., he started screaming at the top of his lungs. Rubbing his back, I tried to calm him down, but that didn't work. Getting up, pacing the floor, that didn't work, either. He was screaming so loud, it gave me a headache. I didn't know anything about being a mother. Summer came back into the room and grabbed Jr. from me, and he instantly stopped crying. That was weird as fuck. Maybe he sensed I was having a baby.

"Damn, girl, what did you do to my baby? He was crying like somebody was killing him. Yes, he was," she cooed at Jr.

"I didn't do anything to him. I didn't know what was going on."

She gave me the side-eye. "Let me find out you pregnant." She walked over and sat next to me.

"Guilty as charged. We found out this morning," I told her, and she started jumping up and down, almost dropping Jr. in the process.

"I'm about to be an auntie!" she sang and rubbed my stomach.

We started talking, and Summer was more excited than I was, but I still had my doubts. I didn't want to end up like my mother, but she assured me she would be there for me every step of the way. The bond we had, no one could break. Starting to feel nauseous, I ran to the bathroom and threw up everything I had eaten earlier. Summer held my hair and rubbed my back. Yeah, this was about to be a long pregnancy. Once I was done emptying the contents of my stomach, I got up and rinsed my mouth out. Summer gave me a spare toothbrush, so I brushed my teeth. We left out the bathroom and returned to the living room. Both babies were asleep, so Summer and I enjoyed each other. I had missed our sisterly talks.

"Sam proposed to me," I blurted, and Summer looked at me with wide eyes.

"Oh my God, congratulations, sis! I'm so happy for you. I'm so glad you found a man like Sam. You know I couldn't stand them other niggas," she laughed.

"Thanks, sis. Sam has come into my life and broke down the walls I had up. He is an amazing man, and I know he is gonna be an even better daddy." I was indeed at a happy place in my life. Sam was it for me, and I wouldn't have it any other way.

We talked a little more, and I started to get tired, so I retired to the guest bedroom. All that loving Sam had given me earlier was taking a toll on me. I needed at least two days to recuperate; he had worn my ass out. Once I texted Sam I loved him, I was out for the count.

Chapter 20

Troy

We had Shaq exactly where we wanted him. While his mother was in the store, shopping, we waited outside for her. We weren't going to do anything to her, we just wanted Shaq, and she would be free to go. I told Summer I was going to the shop, but she knew what was up because I had on all black. She told me to be careful, but she didn't have to worry about me because I was always careful. While his mother was loading the car with the groceries, Sam pulled up behind her and placed a bag over her head. She tried to put up a fight, but we were stronger.

We were cautious because we didn't need to get pulled over. Once we made it to the warehouse, Sam got Shaq's mother out the van and led her inside His mama was feisty; she put up a fight the whole time they were trying to get her inside. Taking the bag off her head, she was about to scream, and I shook my head. It wasn't going to do any good for her to scream because we were in a secluded area.

"Listen, we are not gonna hurt you, we just want your son. He has done some bad things to people I love, so bring him to us, and you are free to go." If looks could kill, I would be a dead motherfucker.

"I ain't doing a damn thing. Let me go, and I won't tell the police on y'all." I had to laugh at her ass; we weren't scared of the damn police. Hell, we had most of them motherfuckers on our payroll, so we were good.

"Ma'am, no disrespect, but we don't give a fuck about the damn police. Half of their asses are on our payroll anyway." She looked at me with wide eyes.

"Does my son owe you money? I can give you that money, please, just let us go. I promise none of this will be spoken of." She looked scared as hell, but it wasn't about any money. I told her what he had done.

All she had to do was tell us where her son was, or bring him to us, but she was making this shit harder than it should be. We had other shit to do, and she was playing. She was annoying the fuck out of a nigga. All she had to do was cooperate, and she would be free to go.

"So, are you gonna tell us where we can find your son? Or, are we gonna be here all night?" I wasn't going to be here all night; I was going home to get in the bed with my baby.

"Are you gonna kill him? He is my only child. Please, I'll do anything, just don't kill him," she begged for her son's life. She knew the truth, so I didn't even know why she had asked. This woman had to be crazy, but the tears she cried didn't mean shit to me. He was indeed dying, and I was going to go home and sleep like a baby.

"Naw, we just want to talk to him, then we are gonna go on about our lives." I tried to make it as believable as possible. He was going home all right. Yep, straight to hell. This nigga didn't deserve to live another day on this earth.

"I don't believe y'all. I know what y'all do. Look at how y'all are dressed." She looked from me to Sam to Craig. She was starting to get on my damn nerves. She was sitting there judging us, and she didn't even know us. That was where people messed up, always trying to judge a book by the cover.

Then a light bulb went off. I was done talking to her ass. I was going to get Craig to head back to the store and get her purse. I knew her ID had her address on it. Going into the other room, I grabbed a piece of tape and placed it over her mouth. Tying her hands behind her back, I put the bag back over her head since she didn't want to communicate with me. Moving close to where Sam and Craig were standing, I told Sam to watch her and told Craig to follow me because I needed to holla at him. Going into a spare room, I got down to business.

"I need you to go back to the store and get her purse. Her license is gonna take us right to Shaq's ass. I don't know why I didn't think of this before." Craig smiled his ass off, and I knew he had a trick up his sleeve.

"Nigga, you got it. Let me run back up here and get that. I'll be back in a little while." He dapped me up and left out.

In the other room, I heard muffled noises. I knew it was Shaq's mama, but I didn't have shit to say to her ass. I went into the other room and made sure baby girl was OK. When I saw she was still sleeping, I left the room. Sam was standing over in the corner with his eyes glued to his phone, so I knew it had to be Carla.

"Nigga, what you over there grinning at?" I snatched his phone, and he snatched it back.

"Get you some business, nigga. But if you must know, it's Carla. Man, that's my baby. She 'bout to be a nigga's wife soon. I'm tired of playing with her ass." My nigga looked happy as hell, and I was glad he had found someone like Carla. The women he dealt with were gold diggers, but Carla, she didn't care about his money. She only wanted him for him; all that other shit was a plus. Carla was going to be a great wife. Within the short time I'd known her, she'd shown me nothing but sisterly love.

"Word, that's what's up, nigga. I'm happy for you, man." We dapped each other up.

We conversed for a little longer, and Craig came through the door, skipping and swinging the purse. This nigga was a fool. Once he gave me the purse, I emptied the contents out of it. Picking up her wallet, I looked through it and found her license. That was all I needed. I didn't know why I had made things harder than they needed to be. Waving the license in the air, Sam and Craig smiled hard as shit. I was excited as fuck because this nigga wasn't about to cause any more problems. As promised, we let his mother go. I had Craig take her back to the store we had gotten her from. Pulling the bag off her head and untying her, we needed to get her out of here. I hoped this shit didn't come back to bite me in the ass for letting her go. Something told me to kill her, but I couldn't bring myself to do it.

"I'm sorry about the problems we caused. You are free to go. Craig will be taking you back to the store. We don't wanna hear about what happened here, is that clear?" She nodded, and I felt she wasn't going to say anything because she was scared of what was going to happen to her. Once they were out, Sam and I left right behind them.

"Nigga, you ready for this?" I asked as I dapped him up.

"Hell yeah, nigga. I'm just ready to get this shit over with so I can go lay under Carla's fine ass." This nigga was wild. Hell, I was ready for it all to be over so I could be with my family.

On the ride to Shaq's mama's house, it was quiet. I guess we were still trying to process everything that was going on. This nigga wasn't going to be a problem for anyone anymore. I hoped his mama didn't try and call him to let him know we were coming for him. I think she got everything we said loud and clear, though. Somehow, I knew she wasn't going to be a problem. She loved her life too much for that.

Making it to the address, it was in a secluded area, and Sam and I just looked at each other.

"OK, nigga, you take the back, just in case he tries to run, and I'll take the front. Let's try to get his ass out of there without killing him. I got plans for him." Sam nodded, and we headed for the house.

The house was dark as hell. I knew they were probably in there sleeping, but I didn't care about that. Picking the lock, I entered the house, and it was quiet as shit. I made my way through the house, checking every room and he was nowhere in sight. I was just about to make my way back out the house until I heard a noise coming from the bathroom. Taking the safety off the gun, I proceeded toward the bathroom. I waited on the other side because it sounded like he was coming out. Two minutes later, Shaq came out the bathroom and looked like he had seen a ghost. Nigga was so scared, he pissed on himself. Nasty motherfucker.

"You make a noise, and I will blow your head off. Let's go." I pushed him toward the front door, and he didn't put up a fight. Sam saw us walking to the van, so he came and got in on the passenger side.

"Nigga, didn't I tell you I was gonna find you and kill yo' ass? You messed with someone's life who I love."

"Fuck you, man. Do what you gotta do." This nigga was acting bad and shit, but we would see if he was going to act hard when we got to the warehouse.

Making it to the warehouse in no time, we got Shaq out the back. He was acting hard and shit like he wasn't scared, but I saw through his ass. When we made it inside, Craig was sitting in the corner with his gun aimed at the door. "Nigga, put that shit away, it's just us." I laughed at his ass.

"Y'all was about to get a hot one in y'all ass. Looky, looky, what do we have here," he taunted Shaq.

Tying him up to the chair in the middle of the floor, I got my knife out. We were about to have a little fun before we killed him. Running the blade up and down his face, I cut his left ear off, and this nigga was squirming and crying. I wasn't finished, though. I passed the knife to Sam, and he cut one of his fingers off, and his bitch ass was crying like a little bitch.

Moving over to his right ear, I whispered, "If you had let Summer alone, you wouldn't be getting ready to die." This nigga had the nerve to spit on me. That was a bitch move. I grabbed his tongue and cut it out. I was tired of playing with his ass. Calling Craig over, I let him torture him a little bit, but something felt off about this; it felt like we were being watched. Just when I was about to put a bullet through his skull, a couple of masked men came in, and shots started going off. I started dodging bullets, and when I looked to my left, I saw Sam had gotten hit. Grabbing my burner, I began firing their way and prayed Sam would pull through this. Walking over to the masked people on the ground, removing the mask from the last head, I couldn't believe who it was.

To be continued…

CPSIA information can be obtained
at www.ICGtesting.com
Printed in the USA
LVHW01s1528190218
567133LV00013B/1328/P